Gertrude AND THE
PRINTED PAGE

TO MARTY (MARTHA)

I hope you enjoy
my book.
Ordered by your
friend LIZ

Mary Pout
9/14/12

Gertrude AND THE
PRINTED PAGE

STANLEY L. ALPERT

ALPERT'S BOOKERY, INC.

This is a work of fiction. Names, characters, places, and incidents either are a product of the author's imagination or are used fictitiously, and any resemblance to actual persons, living or dead; events or locales is entirely coincidental.

Published by
Alpert's Bookery, Inc.
POB 215
Nanuet, NY 10954

Library of Congress Catalog Card Number: 98-93483

ISBN 1-892666-00-6

This book is printed on acid-free paper. ∞

Manufactured in the United States of America
August 1998

In loving memory of Frieda Goldberg

ACKNOWLEDGMENTS

I extend gratitude to the many faithful friends who offered support, encouragement, and motivation over the years.

Special thanks to Beverly Bierman, Gertrude R. Szyferblatt, Sheryl Lindsell, and Leslie Crowley-Srajek for their input, objective critiques, and assistance.

Thank you to Meredith White for her help in coordinating production.

Special kudos to a wonderful author and editor—Linda Bland.

And with love to Susan and Sharon for just being themselves.

GERTRUDE

AND THE

PRINTED PAGE

ONE

Something is intriguing about an old bookstore, especially when it is located in the most dilapidated section of town. Cast among architectural artifacts, Gertrude's Bookstore stood as a lasting memento of another generation and an unsung reminder of society's forgotten culture. The nation's populace relied solely on cyber-space communication and audiovisual media for all intellectual input, having long ago forsaken the printed page.

Inside the old store, a silent figure stared sadly at the nearly deserted street. Her ailing vision inhibited by the overcast sky, the elderly woman strained to see who was walking in her direction. A slouched figure, in a heavy winter coat and hat, passed the remains of Jack's Confectionery and drew closer. As he braced himself against a blustery gale, the intensity forced him backward. Recouping his energy, the stranger continued to resist the elements and finally made his way to the bookstore's entrance. Turning the handle, he braced his shoulder against the heavy wooden entry and pushed it inward. Inside where the rage of wintry weather abated, the stranger shrugged his large shoulders and removed his weather-beaten hat. With piercing eyes, he focused upon the frail, elderly woman who now stood nervously by the adjoining window.

"Are you Gertrude Johnson?"

Mustering her courage, the woman replied, "I am."

He placed the hat on a nearby rack. "Good," he responded, then rubbed his hands together to revive their circulation. He scanned the book-filled room then turned his attention back to her.

"How may I help you?" she inquired.

Ignoring her question, he said, "I haven't seen a shop of this kind in years." Picking up a dusty book from the nearest table, he leafed through the pages. "Yes, it's been many years."

Gertrude gathered her courage and approached him. "What brings you here now?"

Surprised by her request, he answered, "Why else? To buy a book. Why else does one come to a bookstore?"

"I just wondered. After all, books are not the most popular of commodities these past few years."

"I am fully aware of that fact; that is why I have come."

"Are you interested in any particular title?"

"I require your assistance. I want your opinion."

"Do you like a particular author?"

"I will respect your choice."

Feeling more at ease, Gertrude headed to a cluttered table and removed a single volume. "I am particularly fond of Homer's *The Odyssey*."

"Fine, I will take it."

"But I also have others...."

"I will take this one."

"As you wish." Walking behind the counter, Gertrude totaled the purchase. "That will be $15.95. I suppose you'd like to charge it on the government card."

"No, I will give you money."

"Money...it's been so long, I've almost forgotten what it looks like." Without comment, the stranger placed twenty dollars on the counter and secured the book carefully under his coat. Noticing he had gone to the door and was putting on his hat, Gertrude called, "Sir, you forgot your change." But he exited into the frigid air, closing the door behind him. Gertrude hurried to the window and watched in bewilderment as the man turned the corner. She returned to the chair by the window and was once again alone in her silent shop.

T W O

Gertrude waited patiently for her lifelong friend to sit before she poured tea at a little table near the back of the store. "Sue, I've got to tell you what happened today."

"No, let me guess. They've popularized the sale of books."

"Please be serious."

"Gertrude, whatever you say won't be a surprise."

"I sold a book today."

"You're kidding, of course."

"Not at all. I sold a copy of *The Odyssey.*"

"*The Odyssey?* Why *The Odyssey?*"

"I'm not exactly sure, but a man just bought it." Pulling out the money, Gertrude added, "And he paid for it with real cash."

"My God, I haven't seen any of this in years. What did he say? Who was he?"

Gertrude retold the story as best as she could recall, concluding with, "The strangest thing was, he gave me that twenty and just picked up the book and walked out the door."

"Without the change?"

"Yes."

"I can't believe it. How many years has it been?"

"Too many. I think my last customer was in over three years ago."

"Aren't you glad you stayed in business?" Sue remarked, chuckling. "That poor man wouldn't have had any place else to buy a book."

"That's why I stay open: With nearly every other bookstore and library now closed, I feel an obligation."

"An obligation to what? To a bunch of books? They're not alive. They're just books."

"I can't believe you! These books are all alive; each has its own story."

"Tell that to the world. After all, they're the ones who decided that reading no longer serves a useful purpose. They're the ones who stopped buying or printing books. Wake up and smell the roses, Gert. The world has changed. You, I, and the books are all relics. None of us belong."

"Have faith, Sue, things might turn around."

"Sure it will—but I won't hold my breath."

"Remember, I did make a sale today."

"Big deal. The guy was probably half in the bag. Probably came in here by mistake or on a dare."

"Please, Sue. Where is your sense of idealism."

"It left me years ago when the new government came into power."

"I will keep my store open as long as I live," Gertrude declared, looking around at her books. "I owe it to them; they deserve a better death than this."

THREE

For the next few days, Gertrude displayed unusual enthusiasm. She cleaned and tidied everywhere and tried to place her many books into a logical sequence for display. By Wednesday evening, however, the stark reality once again forged its way into her mind: No customers and no sales.

It was late Thursday afternoon when the door opened and the stranger returned. Gertrude's heart jumped and she quickly inquired, "How did you like the book?"

"The book?"

"Yes. *The Odyssey.* The one you bought last time. Did you enjoy it?"

Without answering her inquiry or changing his expression, he flatly stated, "I desire another book."

"Any particular title or author?"

"You select."

Without questioning him any further, she strolled among the shelves. She studied the various bindings until her eyes fell upon a particular title. "Here is another one of my favorites."

"I will take it."

"But I didn't tell you its name."

"It does not matter. I will take that book."

She moved to the register. "Cash?"

"Yes. I will pay you in cash."

"$10.98."

He placed another $20 on the counter, took the book, and exited without a single word. Gertrude hurried to the window, but by the time she arrived, he had disappeared from sight. Gertrude returned to her chair, stared at her surroundings, and tried to make sense of what had just happened.

FOUR

"You're kidding," Sue questioned.

"No. That's exactly how it happened."

"Twice now—precisely the same?"

"That's what I said. He came in, asked me to recommend a book, paid in cash, and quickly left," Gertrude reported again.

"Do you think he's from a government agency?"

"I'm not sure, but I'm not doing anything illegal. Remember, the law only prohibits new bookstores from being opened; I've been exempt all these years by the grandfather clause."

"What about the selling of books?"

"I can sell only old books. The law prohibits only the printing and selling of new books. My bookstore permit is valid until the day I die."

"I believe there are only two bookstores remaining in the entire country. Yours and the Schneiders'. Correct?"

"Yes. I guess that makes us sort of dinosaurs."

Sue thought for a moment, then spoke, "Maybe the stranger was trying to find a violation, or some way to close you down for good."

"Why would the government be afraid of me? Business isn't exactly booming. No one's knocking down my door."

"I agree, but it sounds awfully strange to me."

"I know, but what can I do? As long as I am alive, my books and store will survive and I will sell to whoever comes to buy."

"Did you ask him any questions?"

"Not really. Everything happened so quickly. He just came in, bought another book, and left."

"Try playing detective; investigate a little. See what you can find out about him if he comes in again."

"I'm not very good at those sorts of things..."

"Pretend you're Holmes or Watson. Put your mind to it; you'll find a way, I'm sure," encouraged Sue.

"I'll try." Sitting back in her chair, Gertrude reflected, "Somehow, I'm not afraid of him."

"Gert. You're too trusting and naive. Grow up. It's a cruel world out there. You can't escape reality through your books."

"I suppose you're right."

"Right? Of course I'm right. Think about it logically. Every bookstore and seller is now gone except for you and Schneider. As the only ones left, you're a thorn in the government's side; once you're eliminated, every book will be gone forever. It was no coincidence the stranger was here." Grasping Gert's hand, Sue continued, "He was here for some specific purpose. No one ventures into this part of the city without a purpose. Think, Gert, you're my best friend and I'm worried."

"I'll see what I can find out if he returns."

"He'll be back; I can almost guarantee it. Call it woman's intuition."

"Perhaps you're right...I'll see what I can ascertain if he returns."

"And don't let your guard down for a single second."

"I promise I'll be more careful."

The following morning Gertrude searched through the telephone book. Since bookstores were prohibited by law from publicly advertising, it took her some time to find the Schneiders' store number. After several rings, a faint and muffled voice responded. "Hello?"

"Is this Schneiders Book Store?"

"Who is this, please?"

"Is Roy or May Schneider there?" asked Gertrude.

"Who is this, please?" the voice repeated, a bit louder this time.

"Please tell them Gertrude Johnson is calling."

"One moment, please." Gertrude waited almost a full minute before another voice spoke. "Gertrude Johnson, is that really you?"

"Yes. Is this May?"

"Yes. I'm so glad you called."

"I heard you had closed. Is it true?"

May Schneider sobbed, "Gert, I can't talk right now. Roy died and I'm involved in settling—"

"I'm so sorry. Is there anything I can do for you?"

"Yes, but I can't talk right now. I'll stop by your store next week. Are you in the same place?"

"Yes—" The conversation was terminated by a click. "May! Are you there?" Hearing no response, Gertrude replaced the receiver and sat heavily in her favorite chair. Though she had only met Roy a few times, she mourned his demise. Her contemplation was broken by the opening of her store door.

The stranger slipped inside. Gathering her senses, Gertrude stepped behind the counter. "Good afternoon, Mr..." she paused, "I seem to have forgotten your name. Could you please tell it to me again?"

The man stared directly into her eyes, then focused his attention on his surroundings. "I want another book."

Redirecting her line of questioning, Gert continued, "Frightfully cold outside. Do you live nearby?" Instead of answering, the stranger walked around the room and inspected the many shelves. Realizing she was getting nowhere, Gertrude thought for a moment. "Did you enjoy the last one?"

"Yes, I did...." He caught himself; unflinchingly he repeated his request for another book.

"Let me think...I believe I have a good one for you." After rummaging through several shelves, she said triumphantly, "Here it is. Have you read *Lord of the Flies*?"

"No."

"An excellent choice and one of my all-time favorites. The book was considered a modern-day classic at one time." She shrugged her thin shoulders and smiled gently. "That was, however, a long, long time ago Things have changed greatly since then."

He took the book from her hand, saying, "I will take it."

"Would you like another one also?"

"No. Just one."

"That will be $23. I'm sorry it's so much, but copies are hard to come by."

He reached into his pocket, withdrew $30, and placed it carefully on the counter. Gertrude was about to offer him change when he strode away. She rushed to the window, but he was gone.

FIVE

During the remainder of the week, Gertrude worked feverishly. Shelves were relined and alphabetized. A spark had been ignited that caused even Sue to wonder.

"Every week he buys a book?" she asked.

"It's been seven straight weeks. I can finally pay my electric bill out of the profits. This is the first time in eons I haven't dipped into my reserves."

"Do you trust him?"

"I guess so. If he was from the government, he could have given me a hard time from day one."

"Has he said anything that would give a hint of his background or job?"

"Not a single word."

"Either he's extremely shrewd or...well, I don't know," mused Sue.

"He's certainly not stupid...and yet, something tells me there's more to this than purchasing a few books."

"You're probably right; just be careful."

"My God, May Schneider, is that you?" asked Gert as she saw her friend enter the store.

"Yes, Gert, it's certainly been a long time. Too long." The other elderly woman sat. "I'm sorry I've taken so long in getting back to you, but my world has been turned upside down. Roy died suddenly and everything is a mess," her voice quavered. "We didn't expect it. It just came so fast."

"Few of us ever have the luxury to plan such things..." said Gertrude, trying to console her friend.

"He died quickly and without pain. More importantly, he died in the store among his books." Looking around, May added, "That's how he would have wanted it, his books meant so very much to him."

Gert took May's hand, "I can certainly understand how he felt."

"I know that...and that's why I'm here. No one except Roy and you ever appreciated the printed page more. I lasted this long only because of my love for him—certainly not for the books. They have caused me great misery and hardship; my life has been molded and hampered by Roy's love for books. Now that he's gone, I can do what is right for me." Fully understanding, Gertrude continued to listen. "You are the only one left, Gert. The only one who really cares about books. My Roy is dead...and you're now the guardian of the printed page. No one else in this entire world really cares. It was only the two of you." May sighed, "I will be closing our shop within the next few days and moving away; I am going to live with my daughter and her family. Rather than disposing of Roy's books, I'd like very much for you to take them."

"Though I'm flattered you would consider trusting me with Roy's books, I'm afraid I don't have much money...." Gert said regretfully.

"Gert, I'm not asking you for money. I'm giving the books to you for free. That's what Roy would have wanted."

Overwhelmed, Gert sat back in her chair and thought for a moment. "I-I don't know what to say, May."

"Say nothing.   The books will be delivered next week. Hopefully, I will be gone by then."

"Can I have an address?"

"I prefer not, Gert. This recent time in my life has been painful; I'd like to begin fresh and try to eliminate the past. I hope you understand."

"I think I understand what you are saying."

Standing, May sounded relieved, "Good. Roy wanted this, and I'm granting his request. May your future be more favorable than his. Unfortunately, his love for books was his downfall, and his desire to keep them alive led to his demise."

Gertrude furrowed her brow wondering what she meant, but decided not to pry.

Glancing at her watch, May looked at the door, "I really must be going. All the best, Gert, and may you find your inner peace."

Gertrude stared as May walked from her store. She attempted to digest what had just transpired but found the task impossible. The events of the past few weeks were becoming difficult to comprehend. Gert picked up a copy of *The Canterbury Tales* and tried her best to lose herself in the stories.

S I X

Sue stopped by the next day and the friends' conversation quickly targeted the Schneiders.

"May Schneider stopped by yesterday," Gert stated calmly.

"Amazing...I just spoke to some of her friends and they told me she was moving away."

"That's correct. She's going to live with her daughter."

"What else did she tell you?"

"Not too much more."

"Did she give you any details of Roy's death?"

"Not exactly. She was in a rush."

"One of my friends told me the government was forcing him out of business."

"The government?"

"Yes. Evidently a governmental agency was doing a lot of spying on his store."

"Why?"

"It seems Roy was selling several newly published books. All anti-government literature."

"Roy Schneider?"

"Yes. According to my source, they've been watching his store for over a year."

"Why would he do such a thing? It's illegal."

"Well, I suppose if one believes strongly in a cause, they'll try anything to get their point across—legal or illegal. That's how he died, for his cause."

"I think I'm missing something."

"He died while being arrested. The agents barged into his store and caught him red-handed with the goods. His heart just gave out from all the stress. He died right there on the spot."

Shaking her head in disbelief, Gert sighed, "Poor Roy."

"Poor Roy? What about May? She witnessed the entire thing. Her husband died right in front of her."

"Maybe that's why she decided to leave the area...."

"Probably."

"And maybe that's why she's giving me Roy's books at no cost."

"My God! You said 'no,' didn't you?"

"Well, not exactly. They're going to be delivered here sometime next week."

"You've got to stop them from coming. What if some of the newly published books are mixed in."

"Maybe you're right." Gertrude dialed May's number but was promptly informed the line was no longer in service.

"Did she leave a forwarding number?"

"No."

"What about her daughter's address? Perhaps we can get the number from information?"

"She didn't give me an address."

Sue was now nervously watching her friend, "What are you going to do?"

"I'm not sure."

"Well you'd better come up with something fast. I'm sure the government will realize where the books are headed. They've probably tapped her calls. Maybe they're already here."

"What do you mean by that?"

"The stranger, of course!"

"The stranger? I don't think he's—"

"Gert, this isn't a game. Roy is dead. The government wants every bookstore closed—including yours."

"I still don't believe the man who buys books from me is one of them," Gert insisted.

"Do you have any idea who he is?"

"No...he didn't answer any of my questions. He managed to avoid each and every one."

"Doesn't that tell you something?"

"I'd better be more cautious about what I say."

"You're not kidding! I don't want you ending up like Roy."

"Neither do I." Thinking for a moment, Gert said, "Funny, I thought Roy was giving me a present; instead, he was opening up Pandora's box. Could I really end up as he did?"

SEVEN

The next morning, with great effort, Gert moved her chair to a strategic location closer to the front window of her store. From her new vantage point, she could easily observe any movement near her shop. Though she attempted to read the last few pages of *The Canterbury Tales,* her apprehension made concentration impossible. Any shadow change or sudden movement caused her to jump, then shake. It was not surprising, therefore, that when she spotted a huge van traveling down the street, her heart pounded wildly.

"Please. Don't stop here," she spoke softly to no one. As the last word emitted from her lips, the vehicle came to an abrupt halt directly in front of her store window. Nervously, she watched as two men climbed downward to the street and headed for her front door. *Please, not here.*

"Hey, lady! Is this Gertrude's Bookstore?"

"Yes it is. May I help you?"

Joking, he said, "Not unless you can do a lot of heavy lifting!"

Confused, she replied, "Then I don't think I can help too much."

The truck driver assessed the thin woman, "The sender didn't request inside delivery. We only have to leave it on the curb. Is there anyone else here who can help?"

"I work alone."

"That's just great!" Speaking to his companion, he groaned, "What the heck...we'll bring 'em in here for her." Then he turned to address Gertrude, "Lady, don't tell anyone or we could get fired."

"I promise—and thank you very much."

It took nearly the remainder of the day before the truck was unloaded. Because the building had no storage area or basement, the men piled the heavy cartons wherever space was available. Boxes sat everywhere, often stacked eight or nine high in the aisles.

"Look, lady, could you sign this receipt?"

"Certainly."

"What's in these boxes anyhow?"

"Books."

"Books! I thought they were against the law?"

"Only the new ones; these are all old."

"I see."

"Would either of you like to take a book home?"

"You're kidding me. What would we do with books?" Instead, Gertrude reached into her cash register and handed each man a five-dollar bill.

"Thanks, lady, I haven't seen cash in a long time. Is it good?"

"I hope so. Otherwise, we're all in trouble."

"Well, we have to go. Thanks again for the cash and enjoy your books." She locked the front door behind them and stared as the truck pulled away. Glancing upward, Gertrude said aloud, "Roy, how could you do this to me?"

EIGHT

Early the next morning, Gertrude began the arduous task of unpacking the boxes. Though overwhelmed when she started, the many familiar titles raised her spirits. Gert found several duplicate books, but it also became apparent Roy had collected diverse and unusual manuscripts. The fact that she neither owned nor had read the majority of the books only enhanced her excitement. Her thoughts were interrupted by the opening of her front door. She shouted from behind a stack of books, "Hello. I'll be right out."

She pushed a box of books aside, and walked toward the display area. Upon seeing the stranger, she suddenly became tongue-tied.

"I see you've gotten some new books," he said.

"Yes," Gert stammered. "They're from a friend."

"A friend?"

"Yes, a friend. Are you interested in buying another book?"

Examining an adjacent package, he asked, "Did you know the Schneiders?"

"Why do you ask?"

"I notice their shipping label on the boxes."

"Yes. They are acquaintances."

"Acquaintances?"

"I know them through business. That's all, just through business." Trying to divert his attention, she said, "Are you looking for any particular book?"

"I hear they closed their store."

"Yes. I heard the same thing," Gert replied guardedly.

"Tragic," muttered the stranger, in what to Gert seemed a genuine tone.

"Roy died and—"

"So they sold you their inventory?"

Forgetting herself, Gert replied, "No. May gave it all to—"

"I see," he remarked, scanning the aisles. "There are certainly a lot of books. All old, I assume."

"Yes. I can only sell old books. It's against the law to sell new ones."

"Is that so?"

Gert began to feel nervous. "So you came for another book?"

"Yes."

"I'll select one for you." Out of the corner of her eye, Gertrude watched him as he inspected another carton. Rushing, she grabbed the nearest book, "I think you'll find this one of great interest."

Without saying another word, the man paid for the book, surveyed the room one last time, and left.

NINE

"Good morning, Miss Johnson."

"Mr. Siffert, what are you doing here today?"

"What else? Don't you remember I'm your mailman?"

"I know that, but it's not the end of the month. I already received my gas and electric bills."

"Surprise, Miss Johnson, you've got mail today—"

"You're kidding."

"I'm afraid not." He reached into his pouch and withdrew five letters. Gertrude took the mail. She recognized none of the return addresses.

"Mr. Siffert, there has been some mistake, these are not—" She cut her words short as her eyes examined the front of the envelopes—all addressed to Gertrude's Bookstore. She placed them on the counter, thanked him for the delivery, and immediately went back to unpacking the newly arrived books.

T E N

"I don't believe it," Sue uttered.

"See for yourself." Gertrude displayed a large pile of opened letters neatly stacked on the top of her desk. "These are just some of them; I've got hundreds more in the back."

"But why?"

"Why? That's a great question: Why me?"

"I can't believe May Schneider would do such a thing."

"Believe what you want. Here's the proof. There have been at least one hundred letters delivered this week alone."

"It makes no sense to me."

"All I know is that she left my store as a forwarding address for her business. I'm getting all their mail."

"They must have had *some* business."

"It appears that way. Each letter is an order for at least one book."

"What are you going to do with them all?"

"I'm not sure what to do. I'd hate to disappoint all these people who have placed an order...on the other hand, I can't do this all by myself. It's simply too much."

"I'll help you get started. Maybe you should hire someone to help out in the store?"

"You're probably right, but where am I going to get someone? Nobody wants to work in a bookstore anymore."

"We'll put a sign in the window and see what happens." Together, the two women labored at filling each order. It gave Gertrude great satisfaction to know others enjoyed and wanted her books. With every purchase, she enclosed a handwritten note commenting on that particular novel and suggesting other books that might also appeal to the reader.

Although more orders were delivered daily, the two women were slowly catching up on the backlog.

"Gert, look at this letter."

"Is it for another copy of *Arrowsmith?*"

"Not at all. It's from a man who wants to sell you his library of books. He included a partial list and it has many titles you are currently missing."

Gertrude read the letter and then checked her cash box. "Let me give him a call and see how much he wants for them." She disappeared into the back and when she returned said, "We made a deal. The books will be arriving next week."

"Did you get them for a good price?"

"Excellent. He'd rather sell to me than have the government destroy them. I assured him his prize collection would be treated with the utmost respect and that I would only place his books to special customers."

"By the way, you got a note from a man interested in the assistant's job. He said he'd stop by tomorrow afternoon and talk to you."

"How did he sound in the letter?"

"Very polite."

"Good. It seems Roy's gift may not have been so bad after all."

ELEVEN

"Did you enjoy the book?" asked Gert of the stranger who had returned once again.

"Yes." Looking around, he observed, "I see most of the boxes are gone."

"Yes, I've been able to get a lot of the books shelved and should put the rest away within the next few weeks."

"Any word from May?"

"No, I haven't heard from..." Catching herself, Gert continued, "No. There would be no reason."

"The book was most enlightening."

"I'm glad. Would you like another?"

Walking to an opened carton, the stranger examined the shipping label. "It's really a shame they closed."

"Who?"

"The Schneiders."

Gert moved to a neighboring shelf. "Have you ever read *Death of A Salesman?*"

"No."

Holding it firmly, she walked to the counter. "That will be

$14.98."

As he strolled around the shop, the stranger abruptly stopped by another opened box. "I'd like another book."

"Certainly."

As Gertrude made her selection, he questioned further, "Did they send you any new books?"

Startled by the statement, Gertrude replied hurriedly, "Everything I've uncovered has been legal. All the books are old thus far. If I discover any newly printed books, I'll call the Ministry of Cultural Affairs. I've always abided by the law."

"I was just curious, that's all. Just curious."

"For your second selection I'm recommending *Moby Dick*."

The stranger walked over and stopped just in front of where she stood. Looking directly into her eyes he said, "That's certainly a strange title for a book."

"Yes it is, but I think you'll enjoy Melville's story line."

"I hope so."

As soon as he exited the shop, Gertrude slouched in her favorite chair and tried to recover her composure. Her deliberation was interrupted by the reopening of her front door. A neatly groomed, young man entered. "May I help you?" asked Gert.

"Yes. I'm looking for Miss Gertrude Johnson."

"I'm Miss Johnson; how can I help you?"

"My name is Austin Mathews. I have a job interview scheduled for today."

"Yes. My friend Sue told me you were coming." Motioning him forward, Gertrude said, "Please sit down."

"Am I here at a bad time? You appeared to be in great thought. I can come back if you desire."

"No. I'm fine. Please come and sit." She studied his stylish clothing and striking features as he pulled a chair over and sat down. "So you want to work here? My first question is very simple: Why?"

Grinning, he answered, "Why not?"

"For one reason, books are not extremely popular at this particular time, and secondly, I cannot afford to pay very much in salary."

"The pay is a secondary issue. I would like to work here for personal reasons."

"I'd like to inquire as to what they are."

"When I was growing up, my father collected old books. As a result, I not only read and reread each one, but also developed a genuine passion for literature." Smiling broadly, he added, "By working here, I'd be exposed to a great number of books. It would literally be a dream come true."

Feeling more at ease, Gertrude delved further. "Have you ever worked in a bookstore before?"

"No—because they're so very few in number, I never lived close enough for the opportunity to arise. Having just moved into this neighborhood, I was overjoyed when I saw your sign in the window. That's why I wrote as soon as I got home."

"Since this would be only a part-time position, I was just wondering if you currently have another job?"

"Yes, Miss Johnson. I have a college degree and work as a computer analyst for a large corporation." Austin leaned forward in his chair, "I would not consider this position a job; I would take it solely for my love of books and the opportunity to work closely with them. In fact, I'll work without any pay if you'll have me."

Taken aback by his response, Gertrude looked tenderly at the young man.

Before she could speak, he quickly added, "Miss Johnson, this would be fabulous for me. I beg you. Please give me a chance. I promise you total satisfaction." He continued, "All my life I've wanted a position like this one. Could and would you find it in your heart to at least give me a chance?"

Gertrude was so touched by his soliloquy and sincerity that she grinned. "The job is yours. Go take the sign out of the window and we'll discuss your hours and wages."

TWELVE

"Sue, this is Gert. Guess what?" Before her friend could respond, Gert hurried on, "I hired someone to help me in the store. It's the young man who wrote to me; he's so marvelous."

"I'm happy for you."

"There's more. He'll work for minimum wage and is also willing to work evenings and Saturdays."

"That will take a tremendous burden off you. Are you sure he can be trusted? Did you check his references?"

"I didn't check because I feel he can be fully trusted. He appears honest enough..." Pausing, Gertrude added, "Besides, I've been making a deposit every day; all he could steal would be a few dollars. I don't really think he's the type anyhow; he's just so perfect."

"Remember what I always tell you: Don't trust anyone."

"Does that include you?" Gert replied.

"No. I'm an exception," answered Sue, slightly miffed.

"I believe Austin will fit into that category as well. He's so energetic, enthusiastic, and possesses a terrific desire to learn the business. It's just great to be surrounded by such vigor and strength. It almost makes me feel young again." Giggling at herself, she went on, "And he loves books. He reminds me of myself when I was his age."

Hearing the front door open, Gertrude bid Sue good-bye and watched as an elderly woman approached the counter. "Do you have a copy of *Walden* for sale?"

"I believe so. Please wait a moment and I'll check." She returned with the book in hand. "I found a copy, it is $15.99. Would you like it?"

"Yes."

"By the way, how did you hear of my store?" Gertrude asked.

"Word spreads quickly. I used to patronize Schneiders' Bookstore, but Roy died. Yours is the only store left. I'm sure you'll see me again soon. Others will also be coming for books; you can be sure of that. You're like an oasis in a desert of illiteracy. Others like myself, who are thirsty for literary knowledge, will quickly find your doors." She handed Gertrude cash for the purchase. Before leaving, she added. "Thank you very much for remaining open. You provide so very much to so very many. May God bless you forever."

THIRTEEN

Things progressed smoothly over the next few weeks. The store's mail-order business increased at a steady rate with both buyers and sellers utilizing her services. With more capital and available manuscripts, Gertrude had little difficulty maintaining an adequate stock and a wide variety of titles. The number of walk-in customers intensified, making leisure time rare for Gertrude. Her relationship with Austin was amiable and the two fully enjoyed their affiliation. She was unceasingly amazed by his dedication and loyalty.

Early one morning, just after she had opened for the day's business, the stranger appeared. As soon as he entered, Gertrude spoke, "Good morning. I hope everything is well with you."

He didn't respond immediately, instead electing to survey his surroundings. Books were crammed into every available nook. "I see things are very good with you," he observed.

"Yes. Business has been good and I might add very hectic."

"Now that Schneiders is closed, you are the only remaining bookstore left in the entire country. That's quite an honor and responsibility."

"That's true. Sometimes I wonder how I can carry it on such

small shoulders."

Instead of acknowledging her sense of humor, he walked up and down the overcrowded aisles. "I see many more titles."

"Yes. We add a few new books on a daily basis."

"Did you say 'new books'?"

Jumping to her own defense, Gertrude replied, "I mean new stock. I told you before, we do not carry any newly published books."

"I see."

Trying to change the subject, she said, "I am expecting a very special book I'd like you to read. I will require either your phone number or address to inform you of its arrival."

"No."

"No? To which one?"

"No to both. I will be in when I'm ready. Just put the book aside for me."

"Do you want anything special today?"

"Just select two for me."

"Did you enjoy my last recommendations?" Instead of responding, he headed into a book-cluttered alcove. Gertrude followed him and stood at his side. Mustering all her courage, she asked, "Could you please reach up and get that book down for me? I'm just a little too short." After taking the book from his hand, she said, "Please come with me; I require your assistance." He followed and removed another book from a high shelf for her. She handed both books to him.

After paying, he quickly left. Gertrude sat and thought, *Maybe he's just an eccentric. Sue's got it all wrong. He's probably phobic and cannot be around crowds.* Feeling suddenly sorry for the stranger, she thought, *That's probably it; the poor fellow is just very shy.*

F O U R T E E N

"Austin, I'd like to speak to you for a moment."

"Yes, Miss Johnson." A worried expression filled his face. "Did I do something wrong?"

"Not at all; please sit down." Once both were settled, she continued, "First of all, I want you to stop calling me Miss Johnson. From now on, just call me Gert."

"Yes, Miss Johnson. I mean, Gert."

"Good. Now I'd like to introduce an extra service to our regular customers. I feel a weekly discussion group would help motivate and stimulate more reading. What do you think of the idea?"

"I think it's just great!"

"I'm glad you like it because I would like you to assist me in the actual running of the group. Do you have any objections?"

"Oh, Miss Johnson, I'd be honored. Thank you very much for considering me for the job."

"By the way, Austin, just call me Gert." Smiling, she continued, "we'll begin next week with *The Odyssey.* Are you familiar with the book?"

"Yes, Gert. I have read it several times."

Even on short notice, eight people attended the first scheduled evening session. Most were middle-aged to elderly, tastefully attired, and intellectually motivated. Once everyone was comfortably seated, Gertrude nervously addressed the group.

"Thank you for coming and I hope each of you will feel free to interject your own thoughts and impressions at any time during the evening. Are there any questions?"

Getting no response, she glanced at her notes then proceeded. "Before discussing *The Odyssey* I'd like to mention a few details about the author. Though vague, some facts are known of Homer's background. Scholars dispute his actual birthplace, however the island of Chios is probably the most likely candidate. There is also no bona fide evidence that he was blind. Considerable speculation surrounds whether both *The Odyssey* and *The Iliad* were actually the collective effort of others living during that period of time. However, if you carefully scrutinize the style and philosophy of each, many similarities can easily dispute this theory. With little actually known of his personal life, we have only his two great works to go on. Both have endured the test of time and have acted as benchmarks for many other poets to follow."

Gertrude sat down before the group, placing her notes in her lap, "I'd like to now open the floor to any discussion or questions about the book itself."

"How many years ago was *The Odyssey* written?"

"Probably more than 3,000 years ago."

"Is it true many of the Greek works were oral?"

"Yes. In fact, many propose that Homer himself was a professional bard and that his two great works were also oral."

"I noticed a great deal of repetition; was that a common practice in those days?"

"Yes."

"I felt after reading the book that Odysseus possessed almost a dual personality. Am I correct?"

"An excellent observation. He was homesick and strongly desired to join his wife; on the other hand, he was a solitary wayfarer in search of new adventures. Two different faces within the same man."

For the next two hours the group discussed the book in detail. Gertrude had no difficulty in either answering the questions, or directing the flow of the discussion.

"Gert, I have another question."

"Yes, Morris, what is it?"

"Odysseus and his men reached the land of the Lotus Eaters. Does anyone have any idea where that was supposedly located?"

Perplexed, Gertrude replied, "I do not recall reading anything on the subject. Does anyone know the answer?"

Austin spoke up softly, "Many historians and researchers contend that the land of the Lotus Eaters was located in North Africa. This conjecture is based on the fact that several narcotic poppy plants are indigenous to that region. Of course, that kind of mystical flora is more fictional than fact."

Turning to another participant who had previously asked another unanswered question, Austin continued, "The name of Odysseus' dog was Argus and he died in Book Seventeen."

After the group departed, Gertrude was thrilled with the results: They had selected their next book for discussion and eagerly agreed to meet regularly. As she and Austin were picking up, she inquired, "Tell me, Austin, how did you know so much about the book? Your ability to remember details was exceptional."

"It was one of my father's books; I read it many times while growing up."

"You have an amazing power of recall and logic."

"Thank you, Gert." Hesitating, he added, "I was wondering if I might have tomorrow evening off? Something important has come up.

"Certainly." She then smiled. "Do you have a date with anyone I know?"

Blushing, he responded quickly, "No. My sister has come into town for a one-day visit and I'd like to spend some time with her."

"That's lovely. Enjoy your evening."
"If you think you cannot get along, I'll cancel seeing her."
"Absolutely not. Everything will be just fine."
"Thank you very much, Gert, and have a good night."

FIFTEEN

"Good morning, Miss Johnson."

Looking up from her desk, Gertrude replied, "Why good morning, Mr. Siffert."

"Judging from today's mail, it seems business is getting busier."

"You can say that again!"

"Rumor has it you're thinking of expanding..." Mr. Siffert prodded.

Gertrude obliged him. "It's not rumor, Mr. Siffert. I'll be taking over the empty space in the next building; I need a bigger area for my books."

"I can't believe what's happened here."

"Neither can I." He handed her several parcels of letters and left. She placed them on her desk and began sorting older correspondence. With two of Austin's friends working during the day, Gertrude had more time to devote to business operations of the shop. Though she sorely missed her customer contact, she realized other details had to be handled to ensure a steady and systematic growth.

Shortly before noon, a uniformed officer of the Cultural

Ministry entered the shop. Gertrude stood and quickly strode over to greet her, "May I help you?"

"Yes. Are you Miss Johnson?" Gert nodded. "My name is Captain Clifton. I'm from the Forms and Applications Department of Sector 35." Holding up several pieces of paper, she continued, "I have your application for business expansion. I need several more pieces of information before it can be approved." Gert led her to her office.

When they were both seated, Gert asked, "What do you require?"

"What is your reason for wanting to expand?"

"I require more space for storage and retail business."

"Have you been paying your taxes regularly?" Gert showed the officer copies of her last receipts and governmental documentation. After inspecting each page carefully, Captain Clifton continued, "Everything seems to be in order."

"How long will it actually take before I get official approval to expand?"

"Everything else seems to be in order. I'll sign the paperwork within the next few days."

"I thought these things took longer?" asked Gert.

"They usually do, but I've been told by my superiors to pass you unless any major infractions are evident."

"Why?"

"I have no idea—but I do not think they're worried about the country's last bookstore."

"Why not?"

"One simple reason: Once you die, your permit expires, and the entire store will be immediately disbanded by the government. All the books will be destroyed and within a short time no one will ever hear of a book again. The orders are already in your central business file. That's why your expansion has little meaning to anyone."

"I see."

"By the way, Miss Johnson, do you sell only old books?"

"Yes, Captain. I know the regulations by heart. This bookstore only sells older books. Anything illegal will be instantly handed over to the authorities."

"Consider your application approved. I'll give you a temporary permit in case any questions arise."

Gertrude thanked her again and watched her walk out the store. Though she was disheartened by the Captain's foretelling, Gert resolved to sell and distribute as many books as possible before everything came to an end.

SIXTEEN

As she unlocked the door the next morning, Gertrude found a note wedged into the jam. She stuck it in her pocket and made her way to her office. After turning on the lights and reading Austin's memos, she looked at the neatly written letter:

Coming to your store is now impossible. There are simply too many people. Meet me at the south end of Muncer Square at 7:00 p.m. with two more books.

She knew immediately who had written the letter.

Surmising her theory about his phobia was correct, Gertrude felt great pity for him and his apparent inability to mingle with people. *Maybe I should bring him some books on phobias and anxiety attacks?*

Two new store clerks intervened her thoughts, "Good morning, boys." They responded with a cheerful reply. She placed the letter into her pocket and began looking for unfilled orders.

It was a few minutes after 4:00 p.m. when she remembered the stranger's letter. Examining it once again, Gert carefully reread each word. No please or asking...just "bring the books tonight." With careful thought, she finally selected two books. She placed them in a shopping bag and glanced at her clock. At precisely 6:00 p.m. Austin arrived for work. With everyone else gone for the day, the two sat and talked for a while.

"What's in the bag?" he asked.

"Oh, nothing special. I'm bringing two books home for a sick friend. She's too ill to come here."

"That's nice of you. I can take them for you if you wish."

"No thank you. I'll probably stay and visit her for awhile. You know how us older folks like to converse."

"Well, I offered..." Austin continued, "By the way Gert, Tim asked me to cover for him tomorrow. He's going away to see his sick mother. I've made arrangements with my other job. Everything is fine with them."

Gert said affectionately, "I don't know what I'd do without you."

"The feeling is mutual, Gert. You've fulfilled a dream." Gertrude looked over at the wall clock. "I've got to go. I don't want to keep my old friend waiting."

"I thought she was sick."

"She is, but she's eager for me to come."

Gertrude picked up the bag and walked toward the nearby square. She saw the stranger sitting alone on a bench. He acknowledged her presence with a nod.

"Did you bring my books?" he asked nervously.

"Yes. I did."

"How much do they cost?"

"Aren't you even curious about which ones I brought?"

"Yes, but I'll see them when I get home."

"Do you live far from here?"

"Yes."

"Would you like to come to my apartment for a chat?"

"No."

"Have you eaten supper?"

"No."

"Can I at least take you out to eat?"

"No." Feeling more uncomfortable, he again asked, "How much?"

"The two books cost $30.00. By the way, I just want to tell you that I'm giving them to you at my cost." He withdrew two 20-dollar bills from his wallet and handed them to her. The stranger stared into her eyes for an instant and then stood.

Gert inquired, "Will you let me know when you want others?"

"Yes," he responded and then walked away.

SEVENTEEN

"I can't believe it," Sue spoke slowly as she gazed about the huge space.

"Wait, Sue, you haven't seen anything yet."

"What could top this? Your retail floor space has almost tripled in size."

"We now have at least one hundred times the number of books as before and the amount continues to grow at a weekly rate."

"Where are they coming from?"

"All over the country. Just last week, forty-three shipments arrived from thirty different states. Most are from family libraries and collections."

"And the government doesn't do anything?"

"They can't. We're not doing anything illegal. We only handle old books."

"How many employees do you have?"

"We hired two more yesterday; that brings us up to twenty-nine."

"How do you handle it? After all, you're not a kid anymore."

"Austin quit his other job and is my full-time manager. Without him, I'd be lost. He handles nearly everything in the store."

"I'm glad to hear he has worked out so well," Sue said.

"He's like the son I never had. All I do is ask and it's done immediately; no questions asked. They all spoil me rotten."

"Where do you get your help? Everyone else is having a problem finding employees."

"Austin does it all. We've had no problems at all in obtaining bodies. When the work gets too much, he goes out and finds them somewhere."

"I still can't believe how much this place has grown..." pondered Sue.

"Come downstairs. There's something else I want you to see."

"There's more? I don't think my heart can take it." Gertrude and Sue waited until the elevator was free and then descended to the basement. As the doors opened, Sue's eyes stared at the sight.

"This is our mail-order division. It was Austin's idea. We have over 100,000 books in stock in this area alone." They strolled among the high shelves. "We receive over 1,000 orders for books every week and the numbers are increasing daily."

Austin warmly embraced Sue. "Welcome to our humble literary market. We've changed a little since you've last been here."

"You might say that. How are you doing?"

"I've never been better in my whole life." Placing his hand gently on Gertrude's shoulder, he smiled, "I owe it all to her; she's turned all my aspirations into reality."

Gertrude replied, "You only say it because it's true."

They spoke for several minutes before Austin excused himself, "Got to earn my keep or else the boss will fire me."

The two women returned to Gert's office and relaxed.

"Has that stranger been around lately?" Sue wondered.

Gertrude responded, "He has not been in the store in a long time."

"Good. I was worried about him. I just didn't trust him at all."

"Don't you think you are being a little hard on him? After all, we know nothing about him," Gert asked.

"You mean 'knew', not 'know.' Hopefully he will stay away forever."

Changing the subject, Gert asked, "Do you know Austin and the other employees hold discussion groups with our customers?"

"That's great. Are they as good as yours?"

"Better. Each of them is absolutely brilliant and their presentations are almost professional. They possess tremendous insight into their designated subject. If you'd like to stay tonight, Tim will be leading a discussion on *Waiting For Godot.*"

"One of my favorites."

"I know. That's why I asked."

"I'd love to, but I must be getting home."

After Sue left, Gertrude met with Austin. "Everything is going smoothly," he reported.

"Good. Are we still behind in filling our orders?" Gert inquired.

"We caught up this morning, but I think Mr. Siffert is getting tired of us."

"Poor Mr. Siffert. He probably remembers my one-letter-a-month routine. It was almost yesterday."

"Today is today and tomorrow will be tomorrow. Things are always changing, Gert. Who knows what next week will bring."

"I can't wait to see. Now get back to work and let me answer some of these letters."

Standing at attention and mock saluting, Austin lowered his voice, "Yes, boss."

"And don't try to soften me up," Gert shot back at him with a smile as he disappeared.

EIGHTEEN

"Gert, you'd better go downstairs," Austin's voice was urgent as he stood agitated at her office door.

"What is it, Austin?"

"There's a woman from the Ministry."

"Okay."

"I'll stay here and work on the orders you are filling. I don't want us to fall behind again," suggested Austin.

Gertrude walked to where the woman in uniform was standing. "Good afternoon, Captain Clifton. Can I help you?"

"Just looking around, Miss Johnson." Surveying the immediate area, she repeated, "Just looking around."

"Is there anything particular you're looking for?"

"Nothing particular. Just looking in general."

"Would you like a cup of coffee?"

"Is that a bribe?"

"No, Captain Clifton. I was just about to have one myself and thought you might be thirsty. After all, it would be rude of me not to offer you one."

"Perhaps you're right. I believe I am thirsty."

"Let's go to my office; it's much quieter."

Austin abruptly excused himself when they entered the office.

"Please sit down. How do you like your coffee, Captain?" Gertrude spoke politely, but without fear.

"Milk and sugar."

"Is there anything specific I can help you with?"

"No, Miss Johnson. I've been assigned to your store."

"Congratulations. I'm privileged to have you."

"I will be coming around once or twice a month."

"Come as often as you wish. We have nothing to hide."

"My job will be to make sure."

"You're in for an easy time. Austin and I keep a close eye out for any irregularities."

"Who is Austin?"

"My manager. He's the one who just left this office."

Captain Clifton nodded. "Yes. I remember him."

Sipping her coffee, Gert inquired, "Why does the Ministry want you here so often?"

"I'm not exactly sure. I was just ordered to rearrange my schedule accordingly."

"Do they do this for other businesses as well?" inquired Gert.

"Very infrequently. We're experiencing a manpower shortage, you know."

"I didn't know that. We'll try to make your job easy."

"We'll see."

"By the way, I was just curious; did Schneider's Bookstore have the same government coverage?" asked Gertrude.

"I do not know. It was in a different district." Taking a deep breath, Captain Clifton continued, "I'd better start my job. Thank you for the coffee."

Captain Clifton and Gertrude toured the entire store. Employees scattered as they approached, affording the officer absolute freedom wherever she went. After finding no violations, the officer spoke. "I'll be coming back within the month. Of course, my visits will be unannounced. Warn your staff if anything is ever found, the store will be immediately closed and violators could face many years in jail. Do I make myself clear, Miss Johnson?"

"Yes, Captain Clifton, but I'm not at all worried. Come as often as you wish. The coffee pot is always full."

NINETEEN

"Those are the rules, Austin. I didn't make them, we simply have to live with them," Gertrude stated.

Shaking his head, Austin probed, "Why did they do it?"

"The government is not obligated to justify anything; they can do as they want, whenever they want."

"It's not fair."

"Sometimes life isn't fair, but what choice do we have? In this case, we have absolutely none. Either we obey or we cease to exist."

"I just don't like the idea of her snooping around."

"Why? We don't have anything to hide...so why are you so afraid?"

"I just don't like the idea of her being here."

"Austin, is there something I should know?"

"I don't understand your question, Gert," Austin replied defensively.

"Don't play dumb; you know what I'm saying. You're much too troubled over this situation. What's wrong?"

Unable to meet her gaze, he meekly answered, "You're right, but it's a long story."

"Make it short and I'm all ears."

"Years ago, during my adolescence, some of my friends and I got drunk and took a joyride in my father's car. Without knowing it was us, my father called the authorities to report the theft. We were stopped and promptly locked in jail. I was forced to spend the night, before my father could come and bail me out. Although the charges were dropped against all of us, the negative experience of that event caused perpetual anguish toward anyone in uniform," he sighed deeply. "That's why I get extremely apprehensive whenever she's here. Despite all my attempts to fight the sensation, it still lingers in my mind."

"Don't worry about Captain Clifton; from now on, I'll handle her whenever she comes. You just take a break or run an errand. After all, I can't afford to lose my manager over such an avoidable thing."

"Thank you, Gert, for being so understanding. I'll try my hardest to overcome my stupid fears," Austin said gratefully.

TWENTY

Throughout the next three months, business continued to prosper. Despite their expansion, lack of space again became the biggest challenge. Finding no other solution, Gertrude offered to buy the entire building from her landlord. Fully aware that his building was in the seediest section of the city, the owner was easily persuaded to make a profit and sell. For some unknown reason, the Ministry expeditiously granted them permission for the expansion. Sitting with her lawyer, Gert asked, "Why did they approve it so quickly?"

"They have nothing to lose and everything to gain. Remember, once you die, everything becomes the property of the state. You're actually saving them a great deal of time and trouble."

"How's that?"

"Most of the country's books are becoming centrally located in your store. Disposing of them is going to be a breeze when you're gone. Why else would they do it?"

"What can I do to stop them?"

"Nothing. Your license terminates upon your death and it can't be passed along or sold to anyone else. They've got it all planned out. Just a neat little package."

"It's so depressing and final," Gertrude said glumly.

"You're overlooking another factor. They'll have records of all your sales and a listing of your customers. In essence, you're providing them with all this valuable information. They'll know where to find most of the country's book collections. That's exactly how I see it and there's nothing you can do about it." Trying to cheer her up, he questioned, "What are you going to do with the rest of the building?"

"Several dealers like myself have asked to rent some space."

"I thought you were the only book dealer left."

"I am, but a couple of newspaper and magazine dealers want to occupy space within the same building."

"Are they all licensed?"

"Yes. All are grandfathered like me."

"Good...I don't want you to get into trouble because of them."

"All are honest and deeply dedicated to the preservation of the printed page. We are all that is left. When we're gone, it will be society's turn to suffer."

"I'm afraid I can't fully sympathize with those sentiments."

"Perhaps, Harold, you should try reading one of my books."

"Please, Gert, I don't have time for frivolous hobbies. I work too many hours."

"Did you know lawyers used to read books?"

"That was years ago. They were replaced by computers. Everything I need to know is at my fingertips." Pointing to his computer screen, he said, "I simply touch a button and I can access any case within seconds. Can your books do that?"

"What about reading for fun and enjoyment?" Gertrude persisted.

"I've got television and radio. That's what they're for; I think all day long; when I go home, I just want to relax."

"You're missing a great many things, Harold."

"Gertrude, just because I'm your lawyer doesn't mean I agree with your ideas and values. You pay me to represent you and that's what I do. Keep your books and let me continue to practice law."

TWENTY-ONE

It was customary for the entire staff to meet weekly. During these sessions, Austin discussed any problems or topics relevant to the business. Gertrude sat at Austin's side, though all final decisions of any consequence were still hers to make. Nearing the end of a rather genial meeting, Tim raised his hand. "I'd like to ask Gertrude a non-business question. Is it okay?"

"Certainly, Tim, what would you like to know?" Gertrude answered.

"I'd like to know which is your favorite book and which author you like the most?"

Surveying her staff, she smiled. "Nothing like an easy question." Everyone laughed and waited for her answer. "There are a multitude of great authors and books; I love so many of them equally."

"Give us a few of your favorites."

"Shakespeare, Hemingway, Huxley, Golding, Beckett, Steinbeck, Lewis, Buck, Elliot, and Kipling are a few of my all-time favorites." Looking at the faces of those present, she continued, "There are simply too many to choose from; they're all my favorites.

Each author I carry on my shelves has a small place in my heart. They represent our past, present, and future. All should be treated with respect and dignity. Without any of them, our civilization would and will be lost."

"What about your choice for best book?"

"Impossible to choose just one, but if pushed, I'd pick the Bible."

"An interesting selection."

"Thank you, Austin." Turning to her staff, Gert continued, "I hope my selections meet with your approval." She then clapped her hands lightly. "And now, my children, it's time to return to work." They filed out. Austin and Gert remained behind. "Did you put them up to that?" Gert asked.

"Not really. They were just curious. They do have tremendous respect and admiration for you."

"And I, for them. It's like having one big family."

"That's how we all feel and that's why we're so dedicated to our jobs. You are, indeed, a very special person."

"I feel the same way about each of them—and especially you," concluded Gert.

T W E N T Y - T W O

Gertrude personally welcomed her new tenants to the building. Samuel Harris was the first to move in. As the last dealer of old newspapers in the country, he hoped to ride on the coattails of Gertrude's success. He was independently wealthy so his prime motive was not money. He, like Gert, despised the government's position on printed materials and vowed to keep the newspaper alive as long as possible. Since the printing of new papers was strictly prohibited, only collectibles could be saved by the country's citizens. Samuel aspired to preserve the beliefs and philosophies of his grandfather who had been a newspaper editor. He worked long hours for his chosen mission.

Rebecca Mayweather was the other dealer to rent space. Her specialty was old magazines. Like Samuel, her desire for the conservation and preserving of printed matter far outweighed any risks she might incur. She, too, was the last of her kind. With every other magazine dealer gone, her business was forced to carry on the tradition and sovereignty of the periodical alone. As with the other printed material, the publishing of new magazines was forbidden.

The three dealers represented the last of three dying arts. Each committed their individual lives to the safekeeping of a freedom. Though their interests differed, a cohesion and camaraderie quickly developed.

TWENTY-THREE

"Miss Johnson, may I come in?" asked Gertrude's assistant.

"Yes, Mary. What is it?"

"I hope you won't get mad, but I forgot to give you something yesterday."

"What is it?"

I found an envelope stuck under the outside door yesterday morning. It was addressed to you. I became preoccupied and forgot to give it to you." Handing her boss the note, Mary continued, "I hope I didn't cause any problem."

"It's okay, but please don't let it happen again; it might be important," Gertrude gently admonished.

"Thank you, Miss Johnson, for not being mad, and I promise it won't happen again." Mary returned to her desk and Gertrude quickly tore open the note:

I want two more books. I will be at the same place
tonight at 7:00 p.m.

Rereading the note, Gertrude was swept by feelings of disappointment; the stranger had relied on her for service and she had not shown up at the appointed time. She worried about his reaction and the effect it might have on his behavioral problems. Filled with remorse, she slipped the note in her pocket and made her way to the stacks. With great care, she selected three volumes and placed them in a large paper bag. Gertrude tried to concentrate on her work until 6:30 p.m. when she immediately left for the designated spot—twenty-four hours late.

The bench was empty and so she simply sat and waited. Darkness fell upon the city, but still she waited. A car pulled up and shone its headlights in her direction. "Hey, lady, are you okay?"

"Yes, officer, I'm fine. I was just waiting for a friend."

"You'd better get moving home. You only have another hour before curfew."

"Thank you, officer." She waited another ten minutes, grabbed her bag, then dishearteningly walked to her house. Sleep would not come that night and Gert rushed to work earlier than normal in hopes of finding another note. Disappointed to discover nothing, she returned the three books to their respective locations. She resolved nothing more could be done until the stranger contacted her again.

TWENTY-FOUR

"Gert, I just received the greatest letter," Austin's enthusiasm dispelled her doldrums.

"What is it?"

"First, are you okay? You look poorly."

"I'm fine. I couldn't sleep last night."

"Anything I can help you with?" Austin questioned.

"No. I'll be just fine. Now tell me your good news."

"Our good news is this: I just received a letter from a man in the Midwest. Evidently he owns his town's library and wants to give it to us for nothing."

"For nothing? Why?" Gert asked, incredulous.

"Word has spread about our business. He says he doesn't need the money and has no living relatives. Can you imagine, an entire library full of books for nothing?"

"How are we going to get them?"

"Several of us are going to drive out in trucks and bring them back. That is, if you give your approval."

"How long do you estimate it will take?"

"Two weeks," Austin responded.

"Do we have coverage here?"

"It's all arranged."

"You have my blessings. Go to it."

"By the way, there's more." Austin added.

"What better news can I get?"

"He also has a load of old magazines and newspapers if we want them."

Thinking quickly, Gert said, "Bring them back also. We're not licensed to handle them, but we'll give them to Samuel and Rebecca. I'm sure they could use them in their businesses."

"I thought you'd see it that way. We'll leave this morning and should be back in two weeks."

"Drive carefully and I will miss you very much."

Hugging her gently, Austin assured her, "It's mutual. Take care and don't worry about anything." The excursion took less time than expected; the trucks arrived back within ten days. Neither Gert nor Austin had told Samuel or Rebecca about the additional cargo, so both were thrilled by their unexpected gifts. They repeatedly thanked Austin and Gert and then hurried to inventory their newly acquired merchandise. The two owners did not have adequate storage space, so Gertrude permitted them to use unrented space for this purpose. The building was quickly filled to capacity by its three occupants.

TWENTY-FIVE

Captain Clifton seemed to possess an uncanny ability to sense fluctuations; her visits always coincided with a large delivery or shipment out. Gertrude surmised that the shipping companies or trucking firms must supply her with this information.

"Miss Johnson, I see you received an extremely large delivery two days ago," stated Captain Clifton.

"That is true, Captain Clifton."

"Is the paperwork completed?"

"I have it right here." Chuckling, she explained, "Somehow I expected your arrival."

Examining the vouchers, Captain Clifton said, "Everything seems in order."

"Milk and sugar?" asked Gert as they stepped off the elevator and into her office.

"Yes, Miss Johnson. That will be fine." The officer turned a page of the order and remarked, I see magazines and newspapers were included with the order. Were they old or new?"

"All old."

"Do you have a license to carry these items?"

"No."

"Then—"

"They were purchased by my two tenants, both of whom are fully licensed." Reaching into her top desk drawer, Gertrude continued, "I took the liberty of getting you their paperwork. I thought I'd save you some time."

Studying the forms for a while, Clifton at last uttered, "Everything is in order. Thank you for your thoughtfulness."

"Are you permitted to call me Gert?"

"No, Miss Johnson. Regulations specifically prohibit such informalities."

"Just like taking a cup of coffee." Gert's remark caught the officer off guard. "If you want, you can call me Gert when we're alone. Everybody else does."

"I'll see."

Noticing a short gray hair on the officer's uniform, Gert asked, "Do you have any pets?"

"Why do you ask?" Captain Clifton defensively responded.

"Just curious."

"A dog."

"May I ask what kind, or am I getting too personal?"

"No. I have a miniature schnauzer."

"I discovered this among that shipment you just approved." Gertrude handed a book to the officer, who closely examined the cover: *Dog Breeds: How to Care For Each.* After a few minutes, she returned the book to Gert. "I'm not permitted to read any books. It's against the law."

"Even a book on dogs?" questioned Gert.

"Any book. I could lose my job if caught."

"The book might help you in raising the animal...what if you're doing something wrong?" Gert persisted.

"I am not permitted to read—"

"I have an idea: I must go downstairs for a few minutes. I'm going to leave this book on my desk. Since there is nobody else in the room, if someone were to open and read the book, no witnesses would be present. Without a witness, no law would be broken." Standing, Gert added, "Lock the office door behind me; I'll knock before I enter." Gertrude took her time and returned twenty minutes later. Before entering, she knocked loudly on the door. Everything was in its exact place as she sat down.

"I'm sorry I took so long, but I had a few things to do. I hope you weren't too bored." Looking at Captain Clifton, she continued, "I can't remember. Did you say you have a miniature schnauzer?"

"That's what I said." Getting up to leave, Captain Clifton said, "I've spent too much time here already. I've got other work to do."

"It was nice seeing you again and I'm glad you found the shipment was in order."

As she opened the door, the officer spoke once more, "The book you left on your desk was not inventoried correctly. Do you think it might be here when I return next time so I can recheck it?"

"I'll keep it right in my desk to make sure. I'd hate to break any rules. You can check its paperwork during your next inspection. I guarantee it will be here if you need it."

"Thank you for the coffee, Gert."

TWENTY-SIX

In the midst of writing a rather lengthy response to a customer's inquiry, Gertrude decided to take a small break. She headed towards the employee lounge for a leisurely cup of coffee. She stopped outside the door and listened as two employees conversed.

"Pat, I'm having a problem with *Hard Times*. I can't seem to grasp some of Dickens' concepts."

"Why don't you ask Austin?"

"I'm too embarrassed. You know how he expects perfection. Please help me, I'm really stuck."

"Okay. What's the problem?"

"What was the main plot? I'm unsure."

"So are others. One group of scholars thought Stephen Blackwood and Rachael's affair was the primary scenario. Others felt Louisa's life was the plot, and a third viewpoint relied on Gradgrind as the main focal point."

"I'm just as confused."

"So were, and are many others. Remember, *Hard Times* was not a typical Dickens book. It took him less time to write, had fewer characters, and its structure and economy of words were unusual for his style."

"I got the feeling that Sissy Jupe was merely a catalyst. Am I correct in my thinking?"

"Many others, including myself, share that point of view."

Gert turned and walked back to her office. Settling down at her desk, she contemplated what she had just witnessed: Two bookstore clerks were discussing *Hard Times* as if they were literary critics or English professors. The depth of their knowledge and comprehension amazed even the elderly owner. *Where and how is Austin able to find such distinguished and intellectual help? And they were only clerks. I hate to think how much the managers and supervisors know. I must ask him someday how he recruits.*

TWENTY-SEVEN

Several days later, Gertrude elected to work in the mail-order section; sickness had caused a few employees to remain home. With hopes of avoiding a backlog, she decided to forego her administrative duties for the day and fill some of the orders. She looked at the pile of mail. Taking the first piece, she pulled off the envelope. As she dropped it into a nearby trash bin, a fragment of paper caught her eye. Reaching into the bottom of the barrel, she placed it on the tabletop. Recognizing the handwriting, Gertrude frantically searched the receptacle in hopes of finding other portions of the torn letter. Finding none, she studied the page. Though torn, it revealed several distinct and recognizable words:

Dear Gert ... be care ... Roy died becau ... Au ...

Call me at ... Love always, May Schneider."

She reread the words many times and then methodically searched the floor, desk, and bin for the rest of the letter or an envelope. She found nothing. She examined the Orders Filled file, but no card for May Schneider was present. Pressing the intercom, she urgently said, "Austin. I'm in the mail-order section, please come down here immediately. It's very important."

In less than a minute, he was at her side. "What's wrong, Gert?"

"Look at this letter."

He examined the torn paper and looked puzzled. "I'm afraid I don't get it."

"Get it?" Gert raised her voice frantically. "Get it? It's simple. Someone opened my personal mail and threw it away." She held the paper upward as tears formed, "It was from May Schneider. Don't you see? It was from her. Why would anyone do such a thing? It was for me. It was from May."

"Let me take you upstairs and we'll get someone to take over down here."

"Why would anyone take my mail?"

"I don't understand it myself. It was probably an oversight or mistake. I'll check into it tomorrow when everyone returns."

"It was from May," she said in a quivering voice.

Sitting at her side and holding her hand, Austin gently consoled his friend, "You just relax and I'll try to play detective. We'll find the culprit quickly and have them locked up."

"Be serious, Austin, I'm very upset over this. If I hadn't looked in the barrel, it would have gone unnoticed."

"You take it easy and I'll find out what happened. You have my word on it."

The next day, Austin came to her office. "Gert, I'm afraid I've got bad news for you."

"What?"

"I've spoken to everyone about May's letter. No one remembers ever seeing it. Remember, all letters are double-checked by a supervisor. I guess it either got caught in the shredder by mistake or was torn inadvertently."

"Austin, can you totally trust them? Maybe they're lying?"

"Tim was the supervisor on duty. I quizzed him at great length about the letter; he was as shocked as you and I."

"I do trust Tim. After all, he's been with us for quite a while."

"Tim and I go back many years, Gert. I'll vouch for his honesty anytime and any place."

"It was probably just an oversight, as you said."

"I've taken the liberty to post a memo to all employees about opening your personal mail and being on the lookout for any other letters from May."

"Thank you so much, Austin," she murmured. Searching his face, she apologized, "I'm so sorry for yesterday's outburst."

"Gert, you've got nothing to apologize for. We all love you and are very sorry it occurred. I can assure you, however, it will never happen again."

"Did the order arrive in from Holmes today?"

"It arrived earlier. It's being unloaded right now," Austin grinned with anticipation. "Wait 'til you see the books. All the great ones are there."

"I'll be right down." Watching him step toward the door, she said, "Austin?"

"Yes, Gert."

"Thanks again."

TWENTY-EIGHT

"How did I guess you were coming today?" Gertrude asked.

Captain Clifton looked around the office and smiled good-naturedly, "You know it is my duty to inspect new shipments when they arrive."

"Please have a seat and I'll be right with you." Without hesitating, the elderly store owner asked, "The usual?"

"Yes, Gert." After serving the coffee, Gert handed her several forms. Captain Clifton examined them, then the two women walked down to the loading docks. She checked the cartons against the forms. "Miss Johnson, there appears to be a problem here."

"What is it?"

"The invoice states 312 boxes were shipped and yet your receiving voucher only states 311.

Gertrude looked at the slips, then called over her foreman. He explained the problem: "Miss Johnson, there were 311 boxes on that truck. I counted each piece myself. It must have been a mistake on the other end."

Looking at the Ministry officer, Gertrude said, "I trust Mike implicitly, he's been our only foreman. He would have no reason to lie."

"Very well, I'll accept the answer and make the corrections on the forms."

They walked back to Gert's office and closed the door. Gert spoke frankly, "Thank you very much, Captain Clifton. With all the cartons arriving each day, I'm surprised more mistakes are not made."

"Government regulations are very strict and must be exactly obeyed. I'm sure it was merely a miscount on the other end. I'll take care of everything."

"I have a small problem that requires your assistance," Gert said.

"What is it?"

"I received a small shipment of books this week and would like you to review them for me. I'm not sure if they should be classified as new."

"Let me be the judge."

Gertrude pulled several books on dogs from her desk. "I'll leave you alone to evaluate them properly. The door will be locked, so open it when you've completed your analysis."

About forty minutes later the books were neatly piled in the middle of the desk. Smiling, Captain Clifton said, "Gert, they're fine. I classified them as old."

"Good."

"I think I'd like to reevaluate them during my next visit and if you have any others in question, I'd be glad to do the same. After all, that's why I'm here."

"Thank you again, Captain Clifton. I wouldn't ever want to sell an illegal book."

"I must be going." As she left, Captain Clifton paused, "Gert, did you know that the miniature schnauzer was a ratter?"

"No I didn't know that. That's fascinating."

"And did you know it originated in Germany?"

"How did you learn that?" inquired Gert.

"Just picked it up recently." Grinning, the captain continued, "See you soon, Gert, and have a good day."

TWENTY-NINE

Gertrude was about to step into the shower after a long day, when her phone rang. "Hello?" she said.

"This is Austin. You'd better come to the store."

"What's wrong, Austin. Please tell me," Gert asked quickly.

"You'll see when you get here. Please hurry."

"What about the curfew?"

"The police are here now. They'll give you an exemption when you arrive."

She dressed quickly and soon arrived at the store. Austin led her into the basement. "My God! What happened?"

"A pipe broke and flooded the place."

"How much damage was done?" Gert asked.

"Not as bad as I first thought. It could have been much worse."

"What are we going to do?"

"I've called the entire staff and they'll be here soon. We'll work through the night. I expect to be back in business by tomorrow morning."

They were interrupted by a police officer. "I'll need the owner's signature on this form." Gertrude signed the paper. The young policeman handed her a copy. "We'll be leaving now. I left the curfew exemptions on the counter upstairs. Glad we could help."

After he left, Gertrude asked, "What about the books? Were many damaged or ruined?"

"No. The water level was still low enough when we discovered it."

"It was lucky you were here."

"Tim and I were working upstairs and heard a noise. When we came down to investigate, we saw someone climbing out the window."

"Someone deliberately did this?" asked the incredulous owner.

"It seems to us it was done on purpose."

"For what reason?"

"Your guess is as good as mine."

"Did you see who it was?"

"No. He was too fast and our immediate concern was the safety of the books and business."

"What about the police? Did they catch him?"

"We didn't tell them the truth. We only told them the pipe had broken and we needed their help in getting curfew exemptions."

"Why? Maybe they could have caught him?"

"Gert, don't be naive. The police are the government. They don't care about this bookstore or building. We're a thorn in their side. They'll be glad when we're gone." Sneering, he added, "We can't count on them for anything. We'll just have to protect ourselves better."

"I'm not sure what you mean," Gert said slowly, a bit surprised at his tone.

"I'm having bars and a security system installed tomorrow. We've got to protect your interest and investment."

"I suppose you're right about the alarm, but I'm not sure if I fully agree about the police."

"Regardless, we'd better start cleaning up before any more water damage occurs.

Within the hour, her entire staff was present and cleaning the room.

"I guess we were very lucky. I'm glad you and Tim were here," Gert reiterated.

"You can say that again," Austin replied.

"Maybe it was just a burglar?" conjectured Gert.

"Perhaps. But why cut the pipe? If he was after money or valuables, he'd look for them. Why destroy the place?"

"If you are correct, why not leave a bomb?"

"Probably wanted it to look like an accident. After all, a bomb would attract some media attention. It's cleaner this way."

"I guess we'll never know," said Gert.

"Not unless he tries it again."

"The alarm will protect us."

"I'm not going to rely on an alarm or bars. The staff has decided to guard the building at night," Austin informed her.

"I can't ask anyone to do that!" exclaimed Gert.

"The staff has volunteered it themselves. You and this store are their lives. Everything is arranged. We have scheduled shifts, so everyone spends equal time."

"Do you think it is really necessary?"

"Absolutely."

Instead of disagreeing, Gertrude went back to her office and fell asleep on the couch. By morning, as he had predicted, the job was nearly completed and by midday, no water damage could be observed.

Gert called Sue and explained the evening's occurrences and Austin's theories. "Do you think he's right?" asked Sue.

"I'm really not sure. He does make some very good and valid points..." Gertrude pondered.

"If that's the case, why not just give it up?"

"Never. I owe it to all of them; my books and now my staff," declared Gert.

Next she called Sam and Rebecca for a meeting to update them.

After learning the details, Samuel was the first to speak: "I believe the government might do such a thing, but I can't believe they would be so blatant about it."

"Why not? They want me out of business," Gert replied.

"You're not alone. They want all of us out. They're not happy about my newspapers and Rebecca's magazines," Sam pointed out.

Rebecca chimed in, "That's for sure. I've never had more inspections by the Ministry than recently. Ever since I moved into this building I feel Captain Clifton is almost part of my staff."

"If you have nothing to hide, then don't worry," Gert reassured her.

"It's a matter of principle," Rebecca added quickly. "That's all, just principle."

"They don't inspect other kinds of businesses as much," Sam complained.

"Do you know that for sure, Sam, or are you simply speculating?"

"I know it for a fact. Rebecca and I have done some research. We're being singled out for some reason by the Ministry."

"I hear they did the same thing to the Schneiders," Rebecca confirmed.

Gert was taken aback, instantly recalling the ominous fragments of the note from May Schneider., "Are you sure?" she asked, hoping to be wrong.

"I also heard the same thing from another source. Evidently, inspectors visited their store every day. The government made every effort to hound the poor guy," Sam reported.

"Why?"

"Rumor had it Roy was black-marketing new books."

"What I heard was worse: I heard he had actually printed some of the manuscripts himself," Rebecca added.

"I cannot believe Roy Schneider would do such a thing. Why would he take such a risk? It doesn't make any sense," Gert said.

"I can see his motive...again, it's a matter of principle," Rebecca reiterated.

"Some principle! He got himself killed and the government then took over his business anyway."

"Sometimes I think I'd do the same thing. The thought of a world without newspapers sickens my stomach," Sam commented.

"We all experience similar feelings; however, two wrongs don't necessarily make a right," Gert remarked.

"I can't be so accepting, Gert. The idea of no magazines is very depressing," Sam said.

"Assuming Austin is correct," Rebecca asked, "how far do you think the government will actually go?"

"God only knows, but I'm sure they're giving the three of us plenty of thought."

"I guess you're probably right," Rebecca replied.

"What can we do about it?" inquired Sam. The women's eyes turned to him, when he spoke, "We'd better come up with something; I don't want to end up like Roy."

"Unless either of you has an objection, I'll ask Austin if our staff will also guard your areas at night."

"I think Sam and I would both sleep better knowing our stock is safe."

Sam nodded in agreement, adding, "I do think we'd better come up with other strategies or we're going to be in for a really rough time."

"Is there anyone else to contact?" asked Rebecca.

Sam responded, "I can't think of a single soul. How about you, Gert?"

Shaking her head, Gert said, "It's up to us to find a way to survive. If we fail and the government wins, the printed page will be lost forever."

THIRTY

When she heard the knock, Gertrude looked up. "Come in."

"I'm sorry to disturb you, Miss Johnson..."

"No problem, Mary. What can I do for you?"

"I didn't forget this time."

"I'm afraid I'm missing something..." Gert asked, confused.

Handing Gert an envelope, Mary eagerly said, "I didn't forget the letter today. Remember how I forgot to give you the other one?"

Gert answered quickly, "Thank you."

"It was stuck in the front door this morning, just like the other one."

As soon as her employee left the room, Gertrude carefully opened the envelope and read the brief note inside:

I will be there tonight. Bring two books.

She reread each word several times and laughed, "You're certainly not a man of many words, are you?" Gert continued to stare at the brief notation. *And yet you are exceptional. I'll bring you two extra special ones and I'll be on time.* She placed the message in her pocket and returned to the day's business.

Once her morning meetings concluded, the elderly owner

strolled among the stacks of crowded volumes. She wanted to make up for missing their last scheduled appointment by selecting what she thought were appropriate titles. Scanning an infrequently used aisle, Gert's eyes settled upon two small books. She did not recognize their bindings, so she removed each book and examined their covers. What she saw made her cry out. She dropped the books on the floor and backed away. Austin came running and held the trembling woman. "Gert, what is it? What's wrong?"

"How did they get here?"

Picking up the two books he said slowly, "I have no idea."

"They're illegal! We could lose everything!"

"I'm perfectly aware of the consequences. Please calm down and let's go to your office."

After shutting the door tightly behind them, Gert spoke, "I can't understand this, Austin. How?"

"I'm surprised it didn't happen before. With all the books we buy and sell throughout a single day, I presumed sooner or later there would be a slip-up of some kind."

"But Alpert's books are the worst. Everyone knows they're all prohibited by the government and especially these two! She picked up the books and scrutinized their covers, groaning, "*Animal Tales* and *Bloomingfield* are on the government's hit list."

"Gert, please try to think about this logically: With everything that occurs during a normal working day, titles have little meaning. They're simply words on a cover; books are merely objects of trade. Whether it be an Alpert book or *Kessler's Theory of Population*, it makes no difference to our staff. We've trained them to uphold that satisfying our customers' requests is paramount." Pausing momentarily, Austin added, "We'll just have to tighten our security, increase staff education, and be much more observant."

"What about Captain Clifton?"

"What about her?"

"Suppose she had been the one to make the discovery? We'd all be in a great deal of trouble."

"You can't spend your entire time worrying about every possibility that might occur; if you did, you'd eventually go crazy," Austin pointed out.

Sitting back in her chair, Gert tried to regain her composure. "Suppose your theory is incorrect and someone is trying to destroy our business on purpose. Though you've taken great pains to protect our building, a single deed such as this could instantly destroy all of us."

Austin rubbed his chin and said, "Go on, Gert, I'd like to hear more."

"Perhaps one of our staff members is a government plant?"

"But I—"

"The Ministry has been known to do such things in the past. Why not now?"

Austin stood and began to nervously pace around the room, speculating, "Maybe it was an inside job. Maybe the broken pipe and attempted burglary were simply diversions. Maybe they wanted us to have a false sense of security all along."

"Perhaps it's an elaborate plan, organized and implemented by the government," prompted Gert.

"But I was the one who hired and personally screened each staff member," defended Austin.

"How did you find them?" asked the rapidly tiring owner.

"I knew some of them previously, but most came from recommendations."

"Maybe there's more than one person involved...."

Returning to his seat, Austin grew silent and stared out the window. Finally he asked. "Now what?"

"I believe we should have everyone polygraph tested."

"A polygraph! Of course! That will flush out the culprit. Great idea, Gert."

"We can call in a company and—" began Gert.

"Sorry to interrupt you, Gert, but I just remembered something. I have a good friend who does this as a full-time occupation.

I'm sure he would be glad to help. I'll explain the situation so he'll know exactly how to question each subject."

"Can we trust him," inquired Gert, "with my life?"

"Yes. I mean, we'll have to. He's very professional. "I'll call him right away. I'd like to have him here either today or tomorrow at the latest."

"I'm in complete agreement. Why don't you handle it and get back to me with the results."

"Gladly. Now stop worrying." He arose and took the two books from her desk. "I'll take care of these."

"Please put them into one of our bags. I don't want anyone to see you carrying them around. What if Captain Clifton comes in?"

Placing the banned books deep into a bag, Austin answered, "I'm going to have the staff inspect every shelf and box in the building. I want to be 100% sure no other illegal books are still around."

"I'll feel a lot better when you get the answer to the polygraphs," Gert replied.

THIRTY-ONE

Austin pressed his intercom. "Hello, Gert."

"Yes, Austin."

"Are you feeling any better?"

"A little, but I'm still very disturbed over the incident."

"I understand how you feel. Anyway, do you want some good news?"

"I could certainly use some. Is there any left out there?"

"I spoke to my friend and he'll be coming tomorrow morning. He feels everyone can be tested by noon."

"Good." Gert answered dryly.

"Secondly, we're increasing the defense of the building. After I told the staff about today's occurrence, each agreed to spend more time policing the area."

"It's gratifying to know they care." Pausing, Gert continued, "Austin, what about the books?"

"They're sitting on my desk. I'm going to take them home tonight and personally burn them in my fireplace."

"Has anyone seen them?" Gert questioned.

"No. They're still in the bag and that's where they'll stay until

I get home."

Taking a minute to collect her thoughts, Gertrude asked, "Could you please do me a small favor?"

"Just name it."

"Could you please ask one of the clerks to get me a copy of *Brave New World* and *1984*?"

"I'll bring them myself."

"Don't bother. I'll be leaving shortly. Just put them on your desk and I'll pick them up on my way out."

"Consider it done." After finishing the call, Austin spoke to Tim about getting the two books: "I've got to go help in mail order. Put the two books on my desk, and Gert will come down and get them on her way out."

"I'll do it as soon as I check something at the front counter," replied Tim.

"You won't forget?" asked Austin.

"Absolutely not. Let me go and then I'll get her books."

Gertrude watched her wall clock with impatience; she was worried about missing the stranger a second time. She donned her coat and hat and walked directly to Austin's office. Finding no one there, she took the only bag off his desk and walked out of the building towards her arranged meeting place. She had left plenty of time so she strolled, attempting to enjoy the vestige of the day's sunlight. When she reached the park's entrance, she hastened her gait until she arrived at their predetermined destination. There she patiently waited.

Time passed ever so slowly, but still she remained stationary on the bench. A figure to her far left suddenly caught her attention. The more recognizable he became, the greater the anticipation she experienced. Finally she stood and waited until he reached her side.

"I'm glad you came," he said as they sat. "Do you have my books?"

"Yes. I took a great deal of time selecting these titles. I hope you will enjoy them."

"I'm sure I will," he responded, taking the bag from her.

Sensing the stranger was going to leave, Gert asked quickly, "Could you please give me another moment?"

"I don't have much time."

"Please. There's something I wish to say."

"As you wish."

"I'd like to explain why I wasn't here for our last scheduled meeting."

"No explanation is necessary."

"Yes there is. I don't want you to think I didn't come on purpose. Through a gross mix-up, I didn't receive your letter until the next day. It wasn't my fault."

"As I just said, it is not an important issue."

"But it is! I don't want you to think I'd ever let you down," Gert said adamantly.

He stared at her for a moment. "I will not be able to see you again for quite some time."

"Why? Are you okay? Is anything wrong?"

"Yes."

"Do you need money?"

"No."

"Do you want to buy more books?" Before he could respond to her question, she said, "I could give you a list to choose from."

"These books are fine."

"Then why?"

"It must be."

"Where will you get more books from? After all, I'm the only bookstore left."

"I must do without any."

"Give me an address. I'll send them to you."

"No."

"I'm worried about you. Something is not right; I can sense it." Taking a deep breath, Gert asked, "Are you in some kind of danger?"

"Life presents continuous dangers." He tucked the bag under his arm, then touched her hand. "Yet somehow things always work out for the best. Always think positively and continue your fight."

Gertrude suddenly felt an underlying power this man exuded. He continued to speak, "I must go; others await my arrival." The stranger took several steps and then slowly turned, "I will miss you."

"Won't I ever see you again?" Gert asked.

"Perhaps. Roads often cross when you least expect."

"Please take care of yourself and leave me a note or call if you need anything at all." Without saying another word, he promptly strode to the park's nearest exit.

THIRTY - TWO

Though it took longer than expected, Tim finally straightened out the clerk's quandary. Remembering Austin's request, he collected the two books and headed toward his supervisor's office. Greatly surprised by Austin's presence, he said, "Austin, I thought you had to go downstairs...."

"I did it already."

Tim placed the books on the desk. "These are the ones you asked me for."

"Thanks. Let me call Gert and tell her they're here." Getting no answer from her private extension, he dialed her assistant. After speaking to Mary, he stated, "She already left; she was meeting someone."

"Without her books?"

"I guess so." Surveying his desktop, Austin leapt to his feet.

"What's wrong?" asked Tim.

"Help me look around and tell me if you see another bag containing two books." They searched the entire room, but it was nowhere. Austin dropped heavily to his knees on the floor, his face in his hands.

"What's wrong?" Tim asked again.

"What's wrong?" Austin answered. "What's wrong? Everything is wrong! Gert took the wrong bag by mistake."

"So? What's the big deal?"

"The bag contained the two books I told you about."

"Alpert's books?"

"That's the one."

"Why did she take it?"

"Because I told her the books she wanted would be on my desk." Cursing, he shook his head, "How could I be so damn stupid!"

Tim hurried out the door, "Let me see if I can find her."

He questioned the entire staff, but Gertrude had definitely left. When Tim returned, Austin nervously inquired, "Any luck?"

"None. Some saw her leave with the bag, but no one has any idea where she was going."

Staring at the ceiling, Austin remembered, "She mentioned she has a sick friend. Thank goodness that's all it was."

"I agree. We lucked out again."

"I'm sure she'll tell me about it tomorrow," Austin said nervously.

"Once she sees the mistake, she'll probably dispose of the books herself," said Tim, trying to reassure his boss.

"I hope so. I don't need any more aggravation."

"If she doesn't bring it up, maybe you shouldn't say anything either," suggested Tim.

Austin thought for a minute. "That's probably the best way to handle it. Why get her more upset?"

"And if her friend is sick, no one will ever see the books anyway. They can't be traced back to us."

"Good idea, but the next time I ask for any books, get them here faster."

"Agreed."

THIRTY-THREE

Austin did not hear from or see Gert the next morning so he called her office at noon.

"I've been expecting your call," she answered after recognizing his voice.

"How is your friend feeling?" asked Austin.

"About the same." Pausing briefly, she quickly added, "I may not be seeing her for awhile. She's really quite ill."

"That's too bad."

"Anyway, Austin, what about it?"

Responding nervously, Austin ventured, "It?"

"Don't play games with me. How did it go?"

"I—"

"The polygraph. Is it done yet?" she questioned.

"Yes," spewed Austin, letting out the breath he wasn't even aware he'd been holding. "Jim did them early this morning."

"So?"

"Everyone passed with flying colors."

"Where does that leave us now?"

"We now know the problem didn't originate with anyone here.

It probably means the two books were a simple oversight or human error. I've taken the liberty to begin several preventative programs to eliminate the same occurrence in the future."

"So I guess that's it?" asked Gert.

"I'm glad it turned out the way it did," replied Austin.

"So am I. I'd hate to think how bad it really could have been," the elderly woman's voice was relieved.

"Didn't I tell you not to worry?"

"So you did, Austin, so you did."

"Gert?"

"Yes, Austin?"

"Is there anything else we should discuss?"

"Nothing I can think of. With this issue now settled, we can get back to business."

"Gert, I want to—"

"Want to what? Are you okay?" she asked.

"Yes. I'm fine. I can wait to discuss another minor topic at a later time. It's not really important." Changing the subject, he queried, "How about some lunch?"

"Great idea. I'm starving."

"There's a new restaurant down the street that Tim and I were going to try it out. Want to join us?"

"Love to. I'll be right down and don't bring any money, it's my treat."

Things seemed to settle back into place over the next few days. Just as everyone was comfortably in their routine, Captain Clifton and another officer entered the store. Austin called Gertrude, then quietly slipped out the rear of the building. The owner walked downstairs to greet the Ministry's representatives. "Good afternoon, Captain Clifton."

Without altering her facial expression, the officer sternly responded, "Miss Johnson, this is Major Whittington. Major Whittington is my commanding officer and will take charge of today's investigation."

"Investigation?"

An austere man of considerable height, Major Whittington stepped forward saying, "Yes, Miss Johnson, as sanctioned and duly authorized officers of the government's Ministry, I am here to notify you that Captain Clifton and I will be conducting a thorough inspection of your property."

"Feel free to look wherever you want. We have nothing to hide."

"We'll see, Miss Johnson. We'll just wait and see."

Sensing something was wrong, Gertrude questioned the officer. "Major Whittington?"

"Yes, Miss Johnson."

"How long do you expect to be here?"

"As long as it takes to complete the job."

"I'd like to alert my staff about your purpose. I'm sure they'll feel less apprehensive knowing who is looking around the building."

"I understand and there's no problem, but I must tell you we have been instructed to check everything."

"Everything?"

"Yes. Every book must be examined. Nothing will be omitted."

"That's quite a task. We now have a building nearly full of books."

"We are going to inspect your tenants' merchandise as well."

"May I offer a small suggestion that might save you time and trouble?"

"Let me hear it before I pass judgment."

"If I accompany Captain Clifton and one of my senior supervisors escorts you, I feel a great deal of time could be saved."

"I'm not sure whether regulations would permit such an arrangement."

"I'm not inferring that we would disturb your objectivity or investigation. We would merely guide each of you through our maze of shelving. This will ensure you won't miss anything. I want to clear up this matter as quickly as you do. After all, we have a business to run."

"May I use your phone? I'd like to check out your suggestion with headquarters." Minutes later he returned. "They can find no rules against it."

"Fine. Let me get one of my supervisors; I'll be right back. Please make yourselves comfortable." Gertrude paged Tim. Once he arrived, she shut the door and explained the mission. Tim agreed to work with the Major. After all were formally introduced, the twosomes started the arduous task of inspecting the store's inventory. Captain Clifton was professional; she spoke rarely, preferring to investigate the almost endless rows of books in silence. After finishing each row, the officer would sit and complete her necessary paperwork. Not once in the two weeks, however, did she accept or ask for a cup of coffee. Her mannerisms were coldly matter-of-fact and no overtures of friendliness were ever displayed. The two officers followed their inspection protocol down to the very last detail and never deviated even the slightest degree.

Like Gertrude, Tim maintained a rigid silence and only spoke when questioned. Every new arrival was monitored and each shipment was scrutinized by one of the officials. Nothing was left to chance. By the end of the third week, only a few more rows remained unchecked. Reaching to the topmost shelf, Captain Clifton withdrew a small book and read the title, *James Herriot's Dog Stories*.

"Tell me, Miss Johnson, what is this book about?"

"The author was a veterinary surgeon who lived many years ago. This book, one of the many he wrote, contains fifty different dog stories. It is a most touching and wonderful book."

Looking at its cover, the young officer inquired, "Are you positive this is not a newly published book?"

"Positive. I believe it was published in the 1980s."

"I want you to take this book to your office; I'd like to inspect it more thoroughly at a later date. I want to make sure it meets the standards of the old books classification."

Gert took the book and delivered it to her office. Upon her return, she said, "It will not be sold under any circumstances until you have checked it out completely and approved of its sale."

"Since my assignments do not always concern Major Whittington, I hope my specific request will be treated with the strictest of confidence."

"You have my word; everything that occurs between us will always be treated as such." Not responding to the statement, the officer returned to the task at hand. "Captain Clifton?" ventured Gert.

"Yes, Miss Johnson."

"May I ask you a question?"

"Yes."

"Why are we getting inspected like this?"

Looking around to see if anyone was within earshot, the younger woman whispered, "No one is ever to know." Gert nodded her assent. "The Ministry has received several calls regarding your store. Each specifically mentioned new books were being sold."

"Who would do such a thing? Such lies!" said Gert, straining not to raise her voice.

"All the calls were anonymous. The caller would never identify himself; when asked, he would simply hang up."

"Were the calls traced?" Gert quickly asked.

"The calls were always short, making tracing impossible," explained the captain.

"Are you sure it was a he?"

"Absolutely. I personally heard the tapes."

"So that's the reason for all of this?"

"Yes." Turning to Gert and showing a slight smile, the captain continued in a whisper, "Despite all my objections, Major Whittington and his immediate supervisors insisted on this inspection."

Touching the Captain's hand, Gert whispered, "Thanks for the confidence." After the entire assessment was completed, no violations were discovered among any of the three occupants' inventory.

Major Whittington handed Gert a copy of his report. "Miss Johnson, your store has been found free of any governmental violations. Despite this fact, I have commanded Captain Clifton to increase her number of inspections. Each visit, as usual, will be totally unannounced."

"Thank you, Major Whittington. It was a pleasure to meet you."

As if he had not heard her compliment, the senior official added, "Any transgressions against the government will result in the immediate closing of your business and forfeiting of your operating license." Instead of responding, Gert watched as the two officers completed their work. At last they left.

Turning to Tim, Gert said, "Call Austin and tell him he can come back to work."

"You mean we're done?"

"Only for today; I believe it has just begun."

THIRTY-FOUR

"Austin, what do you think about having a party?"

"Gert, I think it is a wonderful idea. After all, we certainly have a lot to celebrate."

"Those are my thoughts also; the last few weeks have been an ordeal for all of us."

"When do you think we should have it, and where?"

"What about next week?...and here?" replied Austin.

"Here? Why here?"

"It's centrally located for the staff and it's big enough to easily hold everyone." Leaning forward in his chair, he added, "And it's safe."

Gert nodded. "I'll make the arrangements." Word spread quickly among the staff. Laughter and anticipation filled the building as the day drew nearer. Despite being asked personally by Gertrude, both Samuel and Rebecca declined to attend. Sitting at a corner table, Gert watched as the staff and their guests arrived. With over eighty-five in attendance, the room filled quickly with merriment. After the last invited person arrived, the doors were locked and the building tightly checked and secured. Gertrude had spared no expense; food and drink were plentiful. Being the gracious hostess, she walked around the room and mingled with everyone in attendance. "So how is it?"

"Just great, Gert." Tim shouted in an attempt to be heard over the boisterous crowd. "I'd like you to meet my very good friend, Donna." Gert extended her hand as Tim noticed someone trying to get his attention. "Would you two mind keeping each other company for a few minutes? It seems Ralph needs me for some reason."

"It'll be our pleasure," Donna said quickly. The two women watched Tim weave his way across the crowded floor. "Tell me, Donna, how long have you known Tim?"

"We go back many years. Probably at least twenty-five."

"From childhood?"

"Yes. We've remained close throughout all these years."

"What do you do for a living?"

"I work at odd jobs. With a degree in journalism, there's not many positions open."

"What about the government? There's always a demand for someone like you in the Department of Publications."

"I couldn't work there; it wouldn't be right."

"But you've got to earn enough money to live on."

"I'll survive. Lots of odd jobs."

"Would you like to work here?"

"I don't think I could. Too much conflict."

"I'm afraid I don't understand what you mean by conflict," Gert was decidedly confused.

"It just wouldn't work out, but thanks for the offer."

"Did the two of you go to college together?"

"For three semesters only. Tim was forced to drop out."

"Why?"

"His parents were killed in a terrible car accident. He became so distraught that college became impossible. Later on, when things finally got resolved and he was able to straighten himself out, he returned and completed his studies."

"He's such a lovely young man. I'm so glad he works here."

Gently holding Gert's arm, Donna responded, "He's never been happier. You're like a second mother to him and all he talks about is you and this store."

Blushing, Gert added, "I'm sorry if he's too dedicated."

"There's nothing to apologize for; I love him very much and am only glad he's finally discovered something to love besides me."

They were interrupted by Tim's return. "So how are you two getting along?"

Donna gave him a tender hug. "Just fine, we were just lady chatting."

"Anything serious?"

"Just good old-fashioned girl talk. Dull for you intellectuals," Donna teased.

Soon after, Gert excused herself and sought Austin. She found him sitting in the far corner with a couple Gert didn't know. "Gert, I'd like you to meet two of my very special friends." Formal introductions were made and Gert found both to be cordial.

"Gert?"

"Yes, Hal."

"How have you been able to put up with Austin all this time?" Everyone laughed.

"It's been difficult, but someone had to do it," Gert finally replied, smiling at Austin.

Edith interrupted, "I think this is the longest-lasting job he's ever had."

Austin decided it was time to speak up in his own defense: "I wouldn't talk if I was either one of you guys; at least I work for a living."

"We do, but not for a big company."

Gertrude inquired, "What do you do?"

Edith was the first to respond: "We work at odd jobs. With degrees in journalism, there's not too many positions out there."

Gert probed further, though struck by the coincidental

response, "What about working for the government?"

Hal continued. "We couldn't work for them; it wouldn't be right."

"How do you earn enough to live on?"

"I just told you; we do all sorts of different jobs. Somehow we manage to get by."

Noting that the three appeared uncomfortable by her questioning, she shifted to another topic. "We could always use you here. Are either of you interested in a position?"

Glancing at Austin, Edith responded, "It wouldn't work out, but thanks for asking." Austin excused himself and moved to where Tim and Donna were standing.

"I'm just curious. How's Austin's sister?" Gert asked Edith and Hal after he was out of earshot.

"His sister? He has a brother...." Hal responded vaguely.

"Yes, his sister. Austin told me just yesterday she was extremely ill."

"Oh, yes," Edith said. "She's still very ill."

"I don't know her name. Have you ever met her? Does she look like Austin?" continued Gert.

"No," Hal responded. "Her name is Iris and she lives on the other side of the country. We've never met her."

"Austin told me she might be coming to visit him once she's feeling better. He said she's never been to the big city and wants to see it," Gert said.

"That's exactly what he said to us; she's just dying to see the big city." Hal replied.

Gert was about to ask another question when Austin returned.

"Gert, please come with me."

Looking closely at the three young people, Gert protested, "But we were just having a little chat." At last she relented.

Austin led her to the center of the room. As the lights dimmed, Donna and Tim walked forward with an enormous, candle-filled cake. Everyone watched silently as Austin raised his glass. "Gert, on behalf of your entire staff, we would like to thank you for pro-

viding us with a new beginning. To you I raise my glass and drink."
After everyone finished their toast, he continued, "And Happy
Birthday to Gert."

Everyone sang in full chorus: "It's somebody's birthday today...."
Gert was so emotionally moved she broke into silent tears.

A voice shouted from the rear, "The candles, Miss Johnson,
blow them out!"

The elderly store owner grasped Austin's and Tim's hands tightly, and together they extinguished the tiny flames. Pulling Austin
close, she whispered, "How did you know?"

"Secrets are very hard to keep around here, especially one like
this."

"Austin?"

"Yes, Gert."

"Forgive me."

"Forgive you for what?"

"It's not important. Just forgive me." The party lasted until the
wee hours of the morning, but Gertrude was too tired to last.
Shortly after midnight, Tim and Donna escorted her back to her
apartment. There she slept while the celebrating continued.

THIRTY-FIVE

With business prospering even more than anticipated, Captain Clifton visited almost daily. The officer spent a portion of her time inspecting the building's merchandise, but preferred to sit with Gertrude in the privacy of her office. There she would complete her required paperwork and then review her findings with the three owners.

Once this segment of her job was concluded, she and Gert would drink coffee and discuss a multitude of subjects. Though approachable, the young officer still maintained a cloak of professionalism and secretiveness.

"Tell me, Captain, how did you ever get into this line of work?" asked Gert one day.

"I came into it naturally: Both my parents are officers with the department, so after I graduated from the Central Government University, I applied for and was immediately accepted as a reviewer."

"A reviewer?"

"Yes. Our job was to review and censor all printed materials. Anything not in full compliance with the law, was destroyed and banned from the country's populace. We were the first line protectors of our society."

"Like books?"

"All printed matter was reviewed. From advertising to periodicals; everything was checked by the reviewers."

"So you then progressed to your current position?"

"Not exactly. When Royal Head Commander Andrews liberated our country from its past leadership, one of his first edicts was to ban all printed materials."

"I am aware of that fact."

"I only mention it because of its direct effect upon my job."

"I'm sorry to interrupt. It's just that we view the liberation differently."

"Once the law was established, our positions suddenly became obsolete. To protect the country against any new publications, the Ministry developed our current assignments."

"What about your parents?"

"Both hold higher ranks and were not affected by the change."

"Did I ever tell you my parents owned a bookstore?" Gertrude offered.

"No, but I knew it anyhow," replied the captain.

"How?"

"From your file."

"My file? I didn't know I had one."

"Everyone living has a file with the government; it helps us monitor and control."

"Sort of a 'big brother' approach."

"I'm afraid I do not understand the terminology."

"Someday, perhaps I'll explain it in greater detail."

"I noticed you received another shipment from the Midwest, but after I inspected the lot, I noticed another mistake with the invoices."

"Not again!"

"Yes, they do not match. The count is off by one carton."

Let me speak to our foreman."

"I already have. The problem is at the other end. I have notified my superiors and they will continue the investigation."

Concerned, Gert inquired, "Will this affect our status?"

"Not at all. I have assured them everything is fine at this end. As long as you operate within the law, there will be no problems."

"Captain, I am having a difficult time locating any more dog books; they continue to be rather scarce. I believe you have already read nearly every one I have ever handled."

Sitting back in her chair, the Captain said, "I hope you can uncover others; I'm finding them quite informative and very entertaining."

"I'll try harder." Reaching into her top drawer, Gertrude withdrew a thin book. "Here's one on dog breeding, would you like to inspect it?"

"Absolutely. You know the rules."

"I must go downstairs for awhile. Call me at extension 97 when you're done." Before leaving Gert asked, "More coffee?"

"No thank you, I'm fine."

Gertrude kept herself busy for the next several hours. Finally, the phone rang and the owner returned to her office. After saying good-bye to the Captain, she answered correspondence for the remainder of the day.

The next day, she summoned Austin and Tim into her office. "Have either of you seen my copy of *Fahrenheit 451*?"

"No, Gert. Are you sure it's missing? Maybe it's just misplaced," Austin offered.

"I'm positive. I had a copy in my top desk drawer. I was going to send it out today to a new customer. When I looked for it last night, it was missing."

"Was anyone in here besides you?"

"Only Captain Clifton."

Austin jumped. "Maybe she took it?"

"Why?"

"Maybe she was snooping around in your desk and—"

"I have nothing to hide. Besides I trust her completely."

"Trust her?" Austin cried, incredulous. "You can't! She is one of them."

"I understand that, but I still trust her."

Tim added gently, "It seems awfully strange to me. Only the two of you in this room and the book is missing."

"Perhaps I just misplaced it. It's probably just my old age creeping up on me. If it shows up I'll let you know."

Austin responded, "You're certainly not losing a thing, Gert; you're as smart and clever as ever." Looking directly into her eyes, he added, "On the other hand, even if you find the book, it won't change my feelings: I still don't trust Captain Clifton or any other government worker. They're all bad, every one of them."

"How can you make such a statement?" Gert asked.

"I can and will. Don't let your emotions control your thoughts. Be careful, Gert; she's one of them."

THIRTY-SIX

It had been quite some time since she had actually participated in their weekly discussion groups, so Gertrude volunteered to critique *The Scarlet Letter*. Because of her ever-increasing notoriety and status, a larger than normal crowd assembled for her talk. Standing at the lectern before the gathering, Gert experienced a terrible case of apprehension. With every eye focused upon her small frame, she glanced at her notes and then started to speak.

"Hawthorne originally wrote *The Scarlet Letter* as a short story, but his publisher, James T. Field convinced him to make it longer. As an experienced author of short stories, the writer created only four main characters: Hester Prynne, Arthur Dimmesdale, Roger Chillingworth, and Pearl. Other minor characters exist, but they are presented only to enhance these four. Another interesting point is that all the action occurs within a limited geographical area. His vocabulary is strictly controlled and his structure remains tight. Over-punctuation is observed, but is not to be condemned.

"At this point, I'd like to discuss each character in greater depth." For the next two hours, the audience sat spellbound as Gertrude dissected, analyzed, and summarized Hawthorne's famous book. Finally glancing at her watch, she stopped. "I did not realize it was getting so late. I guess I got carried away with Mr. Hawthorne's classic. Before we end, are there any questions or comments?"

The question and answer period became so animated that the session did not end for another hour. Exhausted, Gertrude watched as her staff ushered the last member of the audience from the room. "Gert, you were just great!" Tim exclaimed.

"Why, thank you, Tim. I consider that quite a compliment."

"How did you become such an expert on Hawthorne?"

"An expert? Far from it; I just like to read."

Austin entered the room and gazed affectionately at his boss. "You are a genius."

"Flattery will get you everywhere," she replied.

"No, I mean it. I have read the book many times and yet, you opened my eyes to a great many details I must have missed."

"Who is heading next week's group?"

"I am," responded Tim. "I'll be discussing *Of Mice And Men*."

"A good selection."

"Thank you. Can I go over my presentation with you to make sure it's correct?" Tim asked.

"I'd be honored," Gertrude replied warmly.

"Gert?" asked Austin

"Yes, Austin."

"I have a surprise for you."

"Not another birthday party?" Gert joked.

"No. This is serious. I will be bringing a very special person to see you tomorrow."

"Who is it?"

"I can't tell you that now or I won't have a surprise for tomorrow. I do guarantee you will enjoy his company."

Please give me a hint. I really can't wait," Gert pleaded.

"Tomorrow."

Unable to sleep after her "performance," Gert got to work earlier than usual. Not finding Austin, she went into the basement and helped prepare for the day's activity.

"Good morning, Gert," Austin said when he found her.

Looking up, she said, "Good morning, Austin. So where is my surprise?"

"In my office. He's waiting to meet you." She followed him and was introduced to an elderly, neatly dressed man. "Gertrude Johnson, I'd like to formally introduce you to Dr. Silas Barton." They shook hands and sat.

"It is indeed a pleasure to finally meet you in person. I've heard so many good things about you and your work," Dr. Barton said.

"About me? From whom?"

"Austin and the others. They are constantly mentioning your name."

Turning to Austin, she asked, "Why?"

"I also must say that I found your discussion on *The Scarlet Letter* most refreshing and quite accurate."

"Thank you again. May I ask what your doctorate is in?"

"I have a Ph.D. in English literature."

"I didn't know such animals still existed."

"Like other things, some of us refuse to turn over and die. We somehow survive despite the perils."

"How do you know Austin?"

"He was one of my doctoral students years ago."

"Austin was a doctoral student?"

"Yes. Didn't he tell you that?"

"No."

"Both he and Tim have Ph.D.s in English literature. They were the most gifted and best students I ever had."

"Austin, why didn't you ever say anything?" Gert queried.

"I never thought it was important. Besides, would it have made any difference? I was hired as a clerk, not a teacher."

"I guess you are correct, but—"

"Gert, let me explain why I brought Dr. Barton here today. I'd like to get him involved with our organization and discussion groups."

"I see no reason why not. It would be my pleasure and our good fortune to have you here."

"There's more to it, Gert."

"What?"

Dr. Barton then spoke. "Besides reviewing and lecturing on the classics, I'd like to run workshops and open discussions on newly written works."

"But that's illegal."

Austin explained, "Gert, that's not exactly accurate. The law clearly states the *printing* of newly written literature is strictly forbidden. It does not prohibit or restrict the speaking of words. Therefore, we are completely within our rights to verbalize our thoughts and ideas on these subjects."

"Are you sure about this?" asked Gert cautiously.

"Yes. We've had several lawyers look into the subject and their findings were all the same." Handing her four letters, he continued, "Here they are; see for yourself."

"I don't want to do anything that might blemish or jeopardize my store."

Barton responded, "The last thing in this world any of us wants is to hurt your wonderful bookstore. It is our last beacon; it is the final outpost for literature and the printed page. You have been an inspiration to those of us who humbly sit on the sidelines. No, my dear Miss Johnson, this is perfectly legal. As long as it occurs within the physical boundaries of your building, it is fine."

"Must it be done in *my* building?"

"Yes. That is the law; if it were held elsewhere, it would be illegal."

"Why? Does it fall under my operating license?"

"Precisely. It was grandfathered in with your license and there's nothing they can do to stop it."

"How come I have never heard of this before?"

"We've kept underground until now."

"Why come out of the closet?"

"There is a huge calling by the literary public. They cry out for help while new authors scream for assistance. Someone must offer encouragement and guidance." Standing erect, he said, "Miss Johnson, that is my job as a professor of English literature; it is my responsibility to all of them. I must at least try, for if I fail, others may not follow." Gazing in her eyes, he continued, "In a way, Miss Johnson, you and I represent their last hope. If we jointly fail, then society has itself lost."

Staring at Dr. Barton, Gertrude inquired, "Are you absolutely sure it is legal?"

"100% sure."

"Austin, what should I do?"

"Preserve the word, sentence, paragraph, chapter, and book. The two of you are our only chance."

"I'd like to check with one other person first."

Later in the day, Captain Clifton sat in Gert's office. Behind a closed door, the owner described in detail the proposed program. Though she did not approve of the concept, Captain Clifton agreed it was totally legal and within the definition of the bookstore's operating license. During the week that followed, Dr. Barton scheduled the first of his many discussion groups. Like the store itself, they quickly grew in popularity.

THIRTY-SEVEN

Tim and Austin relaxed during a break. "Tim, have you noticed a change in Gert?"

"Yes. However, since I'm somewhat paranoid, I thought it was just me."

"She's much more sullen and less sociable. She no longer initiates a conversation and is more often keeping to herself."

"Do you think she's ill?"

"I certainly hope not."

"Should we say anything to her?"

"Let's leave it alone for a while longer. Perhaps she can work it out herself."

Gert rested at her desk and gazed out the window. She stared at the crowded street and attempted to recognize a familiar face. Various other stores now filled the once-decaying neighborhood. The buzzing of her intercom brought her back to reality. "Yes? What is it?"

"Gert, this is Austin. Do you have a minute?"

"I'm kind of busy; what is it?"

"We haven't met in quite a while. It's been over two weeks

since our last tête-à-tête."

Gert looked at her calendar. "It's been three weeks! Where have you been?"

Sensing something was terribly wrong, Austin altered his course. "Gert, Tim must cancel this next week's discussion group unless we are able to quickly locate a qualified lecturer. Are you free?"

"No."

"Just no?"

"That's all. Just plain and simply no."

"Gert, is there anything wrong? Are you ill?"

"I am feeling just fine and yes, there is something very wrong." Pausing, she said, "I can just sense it. It has nothing to do with you, me, or the business. I'm very concerned about the welfare of a friend."

Remembering her previous conversations regarding an indisposed acquaintance, he responded, "I understand how you feel. I will take care of things here. Let me know if I can be of any assistance to either of you."

Days later, the intercom buzzed. "Yes, Mary. What is it?" asked Gert.

"An officer from the Ministry is here."

With haste, Gert walked to the basement. "Why, Major Whittington, what a pleasant surprise. I expected to see Captain Clifton."

"I will be doing your inspections from now on."

Trying not to sound too inquisitive, Gert probed, "What about Captain Clifton?"

"She will no longer be doing them. I have been assigned to the task. Like Captain Clifton, I will be here on a very regular basis. Please have your paperwork ready before I arrive."

"Yes, Major. Has Captain Clifton been assigned elsewhere?"

"That is none of your concern, Miss Johnson. Can we please

begin? I have a full schedule." Instead of inquiring any further, she followed him throughout the building. Once he had completed his work, he signed her forms and left. She immediately went to Austin's office. Slamming the door behind her, she stood by his window.

"What's wrong, Gert?"

"You've got to help me, Austin. I knew something was wrong, I just *knew* it."

"Sit down and talk to me. Is your friend still sick?"

"It has nothing to do with her. It's Captain Clifton. Something is wrong with her. Major Whittington is taking her job."

"So?"

"What do you mean by that?"

"Exactly what I said. Who cares about any of them? They're all government."

Pounding her fist against the desktop, Gert countered, "I care and that's all that counts. Out of respect for me, I expect your assistance with this matter."

Taken aback by her outburst, Austin meekly replied, "What do you want?"

"I want to find Captain Clifton and I want to see if she's okay."

"How do we even get started?"

"I know her office number; let's begin there." She dialed the number and waited for the proper connection.

"Hello, this is your Central Inspector's office. How may I help you?"

Speaking in her most pleasant tone, Gert asked, "Captain Clifton, please."

"I'm sorry, but Captain Clifton is no longer working here. Can I connect you with someone else?"

"No. Do you know where I might be able to reach her?"

"Sorry."

"How about her home number?"

"Sorry. I cannot help you. Would you like to speak to another inspector?"

"Is there anyone who might be able to provide me with her home number?"

"I'm afraid all such data is strictly classified. You might try going to the Government's Central Office of Personnel. Perhaps they might help."

Gert hung up in disgust. "No luck." She looked at Austin with a pleading expression, "I've got to find her somehow."

"Let's look in the phone directory."

"She won't be listed. All the names, addresses, and phone numbers of government employees are classified."

"That's right. I forgot." Austin began pacing. "I have an idea. It's a long shot, but it's worth a try."

"What is it?"

"A friend of mine once obtained a copy of the Government's Central Directory. I remember him telling me about it. I wonder if he still has it?"

"Please call him and see." Gert nervously watched Austin for any hint of conversation. She saw him write down several things on a nearby pad and then hang up. "Well? Could he help us?"

"There are three Cliftons listed; General Thomas Clifton, Major Barbara Clifton, and a Captain Dorothy Clifton."

"That's her. Dorothy. The others are her parents."

"Are you sure?"

"As sure as one can be. What about a number?"

"Here it is."

"Did he give you an address?"

Holding the piece of paper upright, he proclaimed, "Ask Austin and you shall receive."

Gert dialed the number and listened. It rang and rang, but no one picked up the receiver.

"Perhaps she went away? A vacation?" Austin conjectured.

"No. She's in trouble. I can sense it."

"Now what?" asked Austin.

Looking at the paper, Gert resolved, "I'm going to her house."

"Right now? By yourself?" Austin asked, worried.

"Why not?"

Grabbing his coat, Austin said, "Let me tell Tim we'll be leaving the building for a while." She agreed and waited. On his return, they exited the parking lot and drove off to the Captain's address. An hour later, they rolled past a tall, modern building.

Recognizing the number, Gert pointed. "That's the one."

With great trepidation, Austin said, "Gert, it's a restricted building. Only authorized personnel may enter."

"Park the car and stay here. I'll be right back."

"Gert?"

"Yes, Austin?"

"Please be careful." She walked directly to the front gate and was immediately stopped by a uniformed officer.

"May I help you, Madam?"

"Yes. I am here to visit my granddaughter."

"What is her name?"

"Dorothy Clifton."

"Yes. I have a listing for a Captain Dorothy Clifton in apartment 3235. I'll ring her for you." Glancing at his name tag, Gert stated, "Please, Lieutenant McArthur. Don't call her. I want it to be a surprise."

"I'm afraid I cannot permit that, Madam."

"Why not? She's my granddaughter."

"Regulations, Madam."

"Lieutenant McArthur, do you know who my son is?"

"No, Madam."

"Have you ever heard of a General Thomas Clifton?"

"Certainly, Madam. Everyone has."

"Do you want me to have to call him on such a trivial thing?"

"I see your point. We wouldn't want to bother him over something so minor."

"And your name is Lieutenant McArthur. I must tell him tonight how helpful you were."

"Thank you, Madam. I mean, Mrs. Clifton. I'm afraid, how-ever, I cannot leave my post. I'll let you in; your granddaughter is located on the top floor."

"Since I have several large pieces of luggage, I was wondering if there might be a freight elevator."

"Yes, Mrs. Clifton. We have a delivery elevator at the rear of the building. It's locked but I'll give you my master key if you promise to return it quickly; otherwise, I could get into a whole lot of trouble."

"I promise and don't be surprised if you hear from the General himself tomorrow."

"Thank you, Mrs. Clifton."

She placed the key in her pocket and returned to the waiting car. "Austin, let me drive."

"Why?"

"There is no time to go into details. Just lie on the floor." Once he was well concealed, she pulled the car to the rear of the building. Leading the way, she opened the back door. They rode the eleva-tor to the top floor, and located apartment 3235.

After getting no response to the doorbell, Gertrude used the master key to unlock the door. As she stepped over the threshold, she spoke: "Hello, is anyone home?" After waiting for a response, they cautiously entered a small, white-tiled foyer. "Hello, is anyone here?" No response.

"Maybe she's not home.... We could get into a lot of trouble: breaking and entering is against the law," cautioned Austin.

"Let's just make sure." They checked the kitchen, living room, and dining area, but nothing stirred. As they entered Captain Clifton's bedroom they discovered her, fully-clothed, lying across her bed.

"Gert, I think we'd better leave. I've got a real bad feeling about this whole thing," Austin said anxiously, never taking his eyes off the Captain.

Gert touched the woman's limp arm.

"Dorothy? It's me, Gertrude Johnson." Seeing no movement, Gert whispered, "Austin, you're right. Something is wrong."

"Look at this." He pointed to a half-empty bottle on the bed.

"What is it?"

"Sleeping pills."

"My God! She's killed herself!" Gert exclaimed.

"Let's get out of here before we get caught," came Austin's first reaction.

"Just check and see if she's really dead," pleaded Gert, now also alarmed.

Austin touched her throat. "I feel a pulse!"

"Thank goodness. Let's find a phone and call for help," Gertrude commanded.

"No! Wait! We can't. How can we explain our being here? Let's just go."

"I will not leave Dorothy like this," Gert said with conviction.

"But think about the consequences! Think about your store!"

"Right now, I'm thinking about her. She's a fellow human being who is in desperate need of assistance."

"She's a government worker. She couldn't care less about us."

Without any discussion, Gert said, "Help me get her into the bathroom." They dragged her flaccid body into the tiny room and induced vomiting. Dorothy slowly came around. "Go make some coffee while I get her into a cold shower."

Fifteen minutes later, Austin was surprised to see the young woman, semi-coherent, lying on her bed. "How is she?" he asked Gert.

"Not good. I got a lot out of her, but I'm not sure what's left. It's probably good we arrived when we did; who knows what might have been if we had come later."

"Did she say anything?"

"Not a word. I'm not sure if she is really out of danger. I've never done this before."

"Neither have I."

"Let's give her some coffee and see what happens." They forced her to drink, but other than coughing, no response was noted. She did, however, open her eyes and stare at her surroundings. The ringing of a phone startled both intruders. After two rings, an automatic answering machine played a pre-recorded message:

"This is Captain Dorothy Clifton. I cannot come to the phone, but..." At the appropriate signal, a message was left:

"This is Major Whittington. Your letter of resignation has been received and accepted. Your final paycheck will be sent...."

Both stared at the young woman. "She resigned?" Gert questioned. "I never heard of an officer resigning. Have you?"

"Never." Looking at his watch, Austin commented, "Gert, it's nearly 7:00 p.m. What about curfew?"

"We can't leave her like this."

"And we can't stay here much longer. Suppose someone comes looking for her?"

"You're right. We'll bring her back to my place."

"Do you know what you are saying?"

"I have no other choice."

"Can I try to talk some sense into you?" Austin pleaded.

"Save your breath and help me take her down the elevator." They gathered a few of the Captain's personal belongings. Austin carried the woman unsteadily in his arms while Gert walked ahead to scout. Neither spoke as the elevator descended to the basement. She dropped the master key onto the concrete floor, then held the door open for Austin. They lay her on the back seat and drove down the alley noiselessly. Gertrude waved to the security guard and chose only darkened side streets for their journey. "Austin, what time is it?"

"Just drive fast. I don't have any passes with me. Curfew will be coming early tonight." They arrived at Gertrude's apartment with only minutes to spare.

After depositing the Captain on Gert's bed, Austin prepared to leave. "Thank you for your help," began Gert, knowing Austin did not fully support her actions.

"I'm very worried, Gert. I still think this is all wrong." Glancing at her clock, she noted, "It's past curfew. Perhaps you should spend the night here?"

"I'll take my chances. Most of the police are busy downtown tonight; there's a big affair of some type."

"I probably won't be in work tomorrow, but I'll call you and let you know what's happening," Gert informed him.

"Gert?"

"Don't say it, Austin, I'll be careful."

It was well into the next afternoon before the almost inanimate body moved. Sitting at her side, Gertrude watched with compassion as the young woman's arms stretched out from underneath the covers. Extending from a fetal position, she continued to emerge until her head and shoulders were fully exposed. Moments later, her eyes dragged open at last. Though glassy, they attempted to focus on her surroundings.

"How are you feeling?" asked Gert.

The question caused Dorothy's head to turn toward the source. Again the inquiry was repeated: "How are you feeling?"

A slight moan was emitted, followed by an extremely weak response. "Where am I?" the woman asked.

"My apartment."

"How?"

"Austin and I brought you here last night."

"Austin?"

"My associate. I was worried about you and went to your home. We found you and brought you here."

The woman turned her head and looked around. "Your apartment?"

"Yes."

Dorothy tried to sit upright. "I must be..." After a feeble attempt, she collapsed backward onto the mattress. "I have to go.

I can't stay here."

"You can't go anywhere in your present condition. You're much too weak."

Once more, Dorothy tried to sit, but as before, she fell backward. The effort took its toll and she fell into a deep, recuperative sleep. Hours later, she again awoke and sat upright. She studied the aged woman sleeping on the adjacent chair; her features were striking, despite the fact she was in her mid-seventies. Gathering her senses, Dorothy stood and quietly extended her arms upward. Recalling the previous events that had led her to this predicament, she moaned. Unable to muster enough energy to walk, she relaxed on the bed and studied Gertrude's appearance. *Why would she help me? After all, I am her adversary. Why?*

Gert moved slightly and then instinctively opened her eyes. Seeing Dorothy, she jolted upright. "I'm sorry. I must have fallen asleep. How long have you been up?"

"I just woke up myself."

"How are you feeling?"

"Very weak and unsteady."

"How about something to eat?"

"I don't want to cause you any trouble. Let me sit for a few more minutes and then I'll be going."

Gert insisted, "Well, I'm absolutely starving. Please join me, I really hate to eat alone."

"Very well, but don't go out of your way for me."

"No problem. You just relax and I'll be back in awhile." Dorothy rested and contentedly inhaled the aroma of food cooking in the kitchen. Shortly after, Gertrude returned. "Let me help you into the kitchen. Everything is done."

They remained silent during the meal. Once adjourned to the living room, Gert spoke. "Feeling any better?"

"The food was excellent and really hit the spot. I guess I was hungrier than I realized." Looking at her wrinkled and grubby uniform, she said, "I must look a sight."

"Who cares? This isn't a beauty pageant. Why don't you go inside and take a nice hot shower while I wash your clothes."

"I couldn't. I really must be going...."

"Dorothy, I heard the message on your answering machine and I know about your job." The young woman started to weep. Gertrude moved to her side and pulled her close in a motherly fashion. "It's not the end of the world. It's only a job; you're young enough to begin again."

Sobbing, Dorothy said, "I can't; it's over. My whole career and future are over."

"Have you spoken to your parents?" At this, Dorothy broke down completely. Gert stroked her hair and tenderly held her within her embrace. After several minutes, she whispered, "Come with me. You need a good, hot shower and I want to get these clothes cleaned."

"I—"

"There will be no arguments. You'll be staying here with me until this whole thing is straightened out." Without another word, Dorothy obediently followed the elderly woman to the bathroom.

THIRTY-EIGHT

"How much longer is she going to stay with you?"

"Austin, she's my guest and she'll stay as long as she needs to be here."

"It's already been three days."

"I'm fully aware of the time."

"Has she said anything?"

"No, and I have not asked."

Sounding frustrated, Austin said, "Gert."

"I know: be careful."

After hanging up the phone, Gert turned her attention to her guest. "Dorothy, we're going out shopping today. We've got to buy you some new clothes to wear."

"But I have clothes."

"You cannot wear your uniform anymore; it's illegal. You're no longer a member of the Ministry."

"I don't have any money."

"I requested that they mail your last paycheck here. The government has already ransacked your apartment and confiscated your belongings."

"How do you know that?"

"I sent someone over there; the security guard informed him of the situation."

Clenching her hands together, Dorothy asked, "What am I going to do?"

"First we're going to buy you some clothes and then we're going to work."

"To work?" Dorothy commented, "I was just fired. I don't have a job."

"I guess I neglected to tell you. You've been hired as my bookstore's official government specialist and mediator."

"I couldn't."

"Do you have anything else at this time?"

"Not really."

"Good, then it's all settled. You officially start your new job today. Right after, of course, we get you some decent-looking clothes."

They arrived at the bookstore shortly after 2:00 p.m. Standing outside, the former government official turned to Gert and declared, "I can't do it."

"Dorothy, you can and you will. Just follow my lead." Upon entering the store, the entire staff stopped what they were doing and stared as the two women walked directly to Gert's office. Before the elderly owner could reach the phone, it rang. "Hello, Austin. I've been expecting your call. Please find Tim and come to my office immediately." Within minutes, the two young men arrived. "Please have a seat. I'd like you to meet Miss Dorothy Clifton. She will be our new government liaison."

Shocked, Austin stammered, "Gert, I...I—"

"Austin, please remain calm and think rationally for one moment. Who else knows more about the Ministry? We have nothing to hide; therefore, our relationship with the government might even improve with Dorothy at the helm."

"Gertrude, I'm not sure this will work," Austin said dubiously.

Ignoring his skepticism Gert looked at the former Captain. "Dorothy, you possess more knowledge than anyone else in this building. You could be an extremely valuable asset to this organization. With Major Whittington inspecting our facility on an almost daily basis, we must have someone on staff who is proficient in the field." Turning to Austin, she continued, "Perhaps, you'd like to do it instead?"

"That was unfair," he charged.

"And so is your assessment of Dorothy Clifton. You have only seen her work in a limited capacity, and yet you have judged her in another. It seems to me she was most effective as an inspector. Am I wrong?"

"But I trained years for that position. This would be all new for me," interjected Dorothy.

"Gentlemen, had either of you ever worked in a bookstore before?"

They looked at one another. "No," came the sheepish and simultaneous reply.

"You were both educated in English literature and yet you've easily adjusted to a new occupation. Retail is not teaching. You were both smart enough to adjust to the situation and grasp new concepts easily. Dorothy is also an intelligent person and has a solid foundation. All she requires is experience and on-the-job training."

"I will try. That's all I can offer," said Dorothy.

"And so will we," commanded Gertrude, catching the eyes of both young men. "Dorothy, you can share my office until we get you one of your own. Tim and Austin, I want both of you to work with her and teach her the fundamentals of our business. Dorothy cannot protect us if she doesn't understand the basics."

Gert sat back in her chair and stared at the three. "Are there any objections to my plan?" No one spoke or gestured. "Good. Take her downstairs and get started. I expect the Major tomorrow."

"How can you be so sure?" Tim inquired.

"We have another large shipment arriving then." Laughing, Gert jested, "You know how these 'surprise' visits work."

Tim and Gert elected to hold their weekly meeting at the luncheonette. After ordering, Gert asked. "How are things working out with Dorothy?"

"Much better than I ever expected. She's bright, imaginative, and highly motivated."

"Shall I congratulate myself now or later?"

"Don't pat yourself on the back yet. She's only been working here for one month. Let's wait and see what happens later on."

"I know, but did you see how she handled Major Whittington?"

"Did I! I think she knows the rules better than he does."

"Remember that was her area of specialization for years."

Chuckling, Tim said, "Did you see his face when she demanded to see his copy of Form 1196 yesterday? I almost laughed out loud when she corrected his mistake. God, did he get flustered."

"Let's not get cocky. Major Whittington is not a man to be taken lightly," Gert warned.

"I'm sure Dorothy will have no problem handling him. She's really great."

"How is she getting along with the rest of the staff?" continued Gert.

"Some are still apprehensive, but overall there are no problems."

"Excellent. She's a good girl; all she requires is some confidence and a little help from her friends."

"I guess she's no different than any of us."

"Any new leads on books?"

"A few. By the way, is Dorothy still living with you?"

"Yes. We decided the arrangement was best for both of us. She will be able to save some money for her future and I will have someone there if an emergency arises." Smiling, Gert said, "We actually have quite a few things in common."

As they walked back to the store, Gert suddenly became serious. "Tim, I have a rather personal question to ask."

"Whatever you want to know about me is yours. Yes, Donna and I are living together."

"Please be serious." Taking a deep breath, she asked, "I want to know about Austin."

"Austin? You already know him quite well."

"I want to know why he doesn't date anyone or have a girl-friend."

"It's a rather complicated and personal issue."

"Please tell me. I worry about him all the time."

"Years ago, Austin was teaching at a large university. He met and fell in love with one of his students. They married and were extremely happy; each lived to please the other. Within a year, they had a son; they lived in a small, off-campus apartment. Shortly after Andrews assumed control, his storm troopers plundered the schools of higher education. Ours was one of the first. Austin was lecturing out of town when they arrived. The entire staff was in tur-moil. Those not arrested scattered like locusts.

"When they found his apartment, they immediately questioned Lena about Austin's whereabouts. Despite all their coercion, she resisted telling them the information they requested." Wiping tears from his eyes, Tim painfully continued, "They raped her and then killed both her and their son on the spot."

"My poor Austin..." Gertrude voice cracked.

"By the time Austin heard the news, there was nothing he could do. He fled for his life and only resurfaced when Andrews restric-tions lessened. It seems our Royal Head Commander stopped wor-rying about the few remaining survivors. Evidently, they no longer posed a threat or problem to his administration. Anyhow, Austin and I studied computers and managed to survive this tyranny."

Shaking her head in disgust, Gert uttered, "Just horrible."

Tim sighed, "Now you see why Austin has no girlfriends or dates. He still mourns the death of his precious wife and child."

"Even after all these years?"

"Some pain never goes away; his feeling of guilt only fuels his suffering."

"What kind of guilt?" asked Gert.

"About being away at the time."

"And that explains his fear of uniforms and hatred for Ministry inspectors..." Gert surmised.

"Precisely. They only revive his past—all of which was negative."

"And Dorothy?"

"In his eyes, she's still a government employee and his hatred will endure forever. Outwardly, he'll tolerate her presence, but inwardly, she only intensifies his anger and hostility."

"Tim, is there anything I can do to help him?"

"You have done more than anyone could have ever expected. You have given him hope. Without his job, he'd probably be dead by now."

By the time Tim had finished his story, Gertrude had to regain her composure. "And you, Tim? How have you been able to endure all of this?"

"Without Donna and you, I probably would have taken the same route as Austin. No man is an island."

She grasped his hand across the table, "I guess my store is more than mere brick and mortar. It seems it is the lifeblood and home to a great many people."

"Gert, how is your sick friend?" Austin asked.

"Sick friend?"

"Yes. The one to whom you used to bring books. You haven't mentioned her in quite a long time."

"She moved away."

"That's too bad. Was she a very close friend?"

"Just casual, but I still miss my visits."

"Did she ever mention anything about the books you brought? Did she enjoy them?"

"I never heard a thing. She hasn't contacted me since she moved.

I assume she enjoyed them. After all, they're not the easiest of books to get. If you recall, I selected each one very carefully."

"I know you did. I remember them quite well. It is so clear it seems like it happened yesterday."

"That's how time is."

"You're so right, Gert. So very right."

Gert looked out her window at the street. "Yes, Austin. I miss my friend."

THIRTY-NINE

Since the very first day of the national takeover, Royal Head Commander Andrews had ordered sweeping changes. Among these were the elimination of every holiday. In their place, he declared his birthday and Liberation Day as the nation's two primary days of quietude and repose. Everything came to a complete standstill. All employees, including those of the government, were required to remain at home or to visit family. Each citizen was ordered to enshrine their exalted leader and expound his accomplishments.

Gertrude placed the required closed notice in the employees' lounge. With business at an all-time high and the store operating long hours, the closing would result in a lengthy backlog. Sitting behind her desk, she contemplated their dire need for further expansion.

Austin quietly entered her office. "I've been talking to the staff. We'd like to come in on the holiday to work."

"Impossible."

"Why?"

"Anyone caught would be either fined or thrown into jail. You know the rules."

"What if we stayed here overnight?" Austin asked.

"Why take a chance? If you're caught, they'll use it as an excuse to shut us down."

"We've got to do something; there isn't enough time to catch up on what we have now. The day off will really set us back."

"We have no choice. We have to close."

"For good old Andrews' birthday..."

"Don't be sarcastic." Gert corrected, then asked, "What are you doing for the holiday?"

"I haven't given it any thought."

"Do you have any outside activities or hobbies?"

"No. This store is my life."

"Don't you think one needs an occasional diversion from one's job?"

"My whole life is this store and its continued success. That's all I require."

"What is Tim doing?"

"He and Donna are visiting a friend."

"Why don't you go with them?"

"It's not a mutual friend. In fact, it's someone I prefer not to see. He's a rather obnoxious individual with a pseudo-intellectual attitude."

"Come over to our place for the day. Dorothy and I are cooking a big supper."

"I don't think so, but thanks anyhow. I'd rather remain at home and catch up on some work."

"Nonsense! I won't take 'no' for an answer."

"Please, Gert. Don't do this to me."

"Why not? You might even have a good time."

"I can't do it."

"Why not?"

"I don't feel comfortable around her."

Pressing the issue, Gert asked, "Why? She doesn't bite, you

know."

"Please be serious and accept my answer. I have my reasons. I just can't come."

"Well, as your boss, I insist that you be there. I have some important work that the three of us must finish. It's exceedingly confidential and can't be discussed here. My apartment is safe from the government's bugs."

"I'll think about it."

"I'll expect to see you at 3:00."

Standing, Austin pleaded, "Please don't do this to me. There's much more to this than you know."

"3:00 on the nose and don't be one second late," Gert insisted.

The doorbell rang at precisely 3:00. "Dorothy?" Gertrude shouted. "I'm busy with the chicken. Go see who it is."

Dorothy opened the front door and discovered Austin standing there with a bottle of wine in hand. "Austin, what are you doing here? Oh! I'm so sorry for being rude; please come in."

"Didn't Gert tell you I was invited for a meeting and supper?"

"No. She didn't say a single word about it." They walked into the kitchen. Gertrude was placing the chicken in the oven.

"I'm so happy you could make it," she said. "There's so much food. This way we won't be eating leftovers for another week." Taking the bottle, Gert said, "Let me cool this off in the refrigerator and finish my carrots. Why don't the two of you go into the living room. I'll be along shortly."

Dorothy and Austin sat on opposite ends of the sofa and remained silent for several moments. Dorothy finally spoke.

"She really didn't tell me you were coming."

"I believe you. I just...well, it's just that I have so much work to do. I really hate to waste the time."

"I know how you feel. I expected to work all day, but Gert insisted on making a big meal. Now I understand why. I'm embarrassed."

"There's nothing to be embarrassed about. You didn't know."

"That's easy for you to say; I still feel very funny."

"Perhaps I should leave?"

"I don't think that would be the best thing to do. I'd hate to hurt Gert. After all she's done for both of us, we owe it to her. She probably did it because she didn't want to be lonely herself. Let's just play along with her little game. It'll only be for a few hours."

"I guess you're right. I could never hurt her."

Minutes later, Gertrude joined them in the living room. "Supper is ready. Come on." Food and wine quickly filled their stomachs. Fully stuffed, they made their way back into the living room where each drank several after-dinner cordials. Barriers were lowered by the relaxed atmosphere and alcohol. Soon they found themselves laughing and conversing.

Gert asked, "Dorothy, how do you like working for us?"

She answered, "I love it. The books and people are just great."

Curious, Austin asked, "Do you miss your inspection work?"

"Yes, I miss it sometimes. After all, it was my life for the longest time. You simply can't forget things all that fast."

"Why did you leave?" Austin probed.

"Austin, please. It's none of your business," Gert cautioned.

"It's okay, Gert." Straightening herself and looking him straight in the eye, Dorothy stated, "I was fired."

"Fired?! I thought you resigned!" came the surprised response from Gert.

"No, Gert. I was fired."

"Why? You were the most dedicated worker I've ever seen in my life."

"I was fired because I broke one of the cardinal rules: I read books."

Austin pushed further, "You were not permitted to read books?"

"That's why I was let go. They found a book in my apartment during one of their routine inspections."

"Inspections?"

"Yes, Austin. Internal Security regularly inspects our homes. All government employees are vulnerable to the actions of that department. They're as ruthless as Andrews' storm troopers."

"Why did you keep a book in your apartment if you knew they might be coming around?" asked Austin.

Taking a sip of wine, Dorothy continued, "During my last visit to Gert's office, I discovered an intriguing novel. While she was downstairs, I started reading it. It was so fascinating I decided to borrow it, read it at home, and then return it during my next inspection."

"*Fahrenheit 451?*" asked Gert.

"Yes, Gert. That was the book."

"Those bastards!" Gert shouted.

Swallowing more wine, Dorothy proceeded, "They found the book and I was terminated the next day. I had no trial, no appeal, and no chance to explain my position." Leaning back against the sofa and looking at the ceiling, she sighed, "The ax fell swiftly and my life changed overnight. All my years of training and work went right down the drain."

"I feel so responsible. I shouldn't have left that book in my office," said Gert.

"It was I who took the book, not you."

Gert uttered, "But why—"

"Why what, Gert?"

"Why did you try to kill yourself?"

Dorothy remained silent and soon began to weep. "Why not? Why not? My whole life was over right before my eyes. My past, present, and future all disappeared. What did I have to live for?"

"What about your parents? What did they say?"

Tears flowing, she answered, "What did they say? They said nothing. My parents refused even to speak to me." Crying loudly now and losing control, Dorothy repeated, "They wouldn't even speak to me. Every time I called, they'd either not answer or just hang up on me." Holding onto her head, she continued, "I have no one left in the whole world. I have no reason for living. I just want to die."

Gertrude rushed to her side and cradled her trembling body within her arms. "You have us, Dorothy, you have all of us."

"Oh, Gert. What's left? I have nothing. I have no one...." Gertrude continued to hold her tenderly, and attempted to reassure her. The elderly woman gazed upon Austin. No words were exchanged. With a thorough understanding of the magnitude of her pain, he stood and compassionately gazed upon the badly shaken woman. Wounds were reopened as he once again was forced to focus upon his own past. Without uttering a sound, he walked out of the room and the apartment.

For the next few hours, Gertrude comforted Dorothy. Finally, she assisted her young friend to the bedroom. Throughout the night, she checked on her status. "Don't worry, everything will work out for you. I promise." She sighed, "I promise."

FORTY

They returned to work a couple of days later. Immediately Dorothy encountered Major Whittington. "Miss Clifton, I have some questions regarding today's shipment."

"Yes. What are they?"

"I've been checking the invoices and noticed that form 75G is missing." Avoiding her eyes, he looked down at the paperwork. "As you are fully aware, Miss Clifton, that form must be present at the time of delivery. Where is it?"

Perplexed, Dorothy stammered, "I'm afraid—" Their conversation was interrupted by Austin's swift entrance.

"I have the form you need. It was inside one of the cartons." He handed it directly to the Major. They watched as he scrutinized every detail. "Miss Clifton, I want to recheck the shipment once again."

"As you wish, Major Whittington, but I must remind you of Article 29, Section 15, Paragraph 42. Any delay without adequate provocation must be—"

"Miss Clifton, I am fully aware of the law, but I suspect something is wrong with the order."

"Again I must remind the Major of the Ministry's exact definition of suspect. It reads—"

Looking with annoyance at the paperwork, he commented, "I guess everything is in proper order. I was just mistaken."

Dorothy did not retreat, but continued her offensive: "Article 356, Section 67, Paragraph 2 clearly states that the government has the right to inspect goods. However, line 18 of that particular paragraph protects the citizen against unnecessary harassment. Shall I quote the line to refresh your memory?"

"Are you accusing me of harassment?"

"No, Major Whittington. I was merely quoting various applicable portions of our existing legal system. Any interpretation or impression that you might have obtained was purely speculation on your part. I remain objective at all times." Slapping the paperwork on the nearest counter, the Major stormed from the building.

Austin watched the exchange with new respect for Dorothy.

"Thank you, Austin, for your help," Dorothy said, as soon as Major Whittington had left. "We would have been dead without that form."

"I discovered it as I unpacked a carton, and realized it was important. Thank goodness my timing was perfect."

"It was excellent, but I thought you had a phobia for uniforms and government workers?"

"I have a strong dislike for them. Someday, perhaps I'll tell you about it." He glanced at his watch. "It's almost noon. How about joining me for lunch?"

"I'm not sure..."

"I'd like to discuss a new project I have in mind. I'd like to make sure it's legally sound and safe," Austin said.

"Okay. Let me call Gert and see if she wants to come with us."

"She's meeting with Tim right now in his office," Austin interjected.

"Maybe they'd both like to come?" suggested Dorothy.

"Dorothy, if you don't mind, let's make it a twosome. I'd like to make up for some of my past rudeness."

FORTY-ONE

Gert's outside line rang. "Hello. This is Gertrude Johnson. How may I help you?"

"Gertrude, it's May."

"May Schneider?"

"Yes, Gert. It's me."

"I'm so glad you called. I received a letter months ago."

"Months ago! I sent you at least a dozen different letters since moving."

"A dozen?"

"At least that number, maybe more."

"But I never received any of them!" Gert was becoming alarmed.

"That's what I suspected—and why I am calling you now."

"I'm so glad you did. I have so many questions to ask. Many things are really bothering me."

"I have an idea what you're going through. Roy and I went through hell just before he died."

"First of all, I want to know—" Click. "Hello! May, are you still there? May, I can't hear anything." Gert hastily pressed her

131

intercom. "Mary!"

"Yes, Miss Johnson."

"I was speaking on my outside line and it suddenly became disconnected. Do you know anything about it?"

"No, Miss Johnson. It's been happening a lot lately on all our lines."

"Did you call the phone company?"

"Three times, and they say everything is working properly."

"How can they say that? This is not normal. Calls shouldn't be cut off like that."

"I will try them again, Miss Johnson."

"And ask them if they can trace the origin of my last call. I want to speak to that particular party again. It's very important that I reach her."

A half hour later, Gertrude spoke to Mary at her desk. "What did the phone company say?"

"Nothing new. The same as before. Nothing is wrong; perhaps lightning hit a wire?"

"Lightning! What about tracing that call? Maybe it would tell us what's really happening?"

"They cannot do it. Evidently only the government and its agencies have that power."

"Since when?"

"According to the supervisor I spoke to, Royal Head Commander Andrews recently ordered the change."

"Just great! If I get another call from a May Schneider, let me know immediately. It's a number one, top priority."

Later in their apartment, Gert and Dorothy sat in the living room and rested. "Dorothy, I've been having some problems with our phones lately. I was just wondering if the government ever taps lines...."

"All the time; it's standard operating procedure. Your store lines have been tapped for years. I'm surprised you didn't know."

"How could I know? I'm not an expert."

"I guess the average citizen doesn't understand these things. Every individual and business that poses a possible threat to the government is constantly monitored."

"What do you mean by constantly?"

"Twenty-four hours a day. Anyone suspected is monitored in every aspect of their lives."

"Are you telling me my apartment is bugged?"

"Yes, Gert. They've been listening and watching you for years.

"What?" Gert cried. "I feel so used, so helpless—and God, so stupid!"

"It's not your fault. You couldn't possibly have known."

"Are they listening now?"

"No."

"How can you be so sure?"

"Because I completely debugged this apartment during my second day here."

"My phone?"

"Probably still tapped. I checked but couldn't locate anything abnormal. They probably tap us from an external source."

"It's a dirty business, isn't it?" a bewildered Gert commented.

"It's a matter of your viewpoint and whose side you're on. By the way, your store is also free from any internal devices. I've been checking continually; everything looks good right now. I would, however, be very careful what you say on your phones. There I have no control."

"I heard Austin took you out for lunch today," Gert said, deliberately changing subjects.

"Yes, we went to the restaurant around the corner. The food was excellent as usual."

"And?"

"And what?"

"How did it go?"

"I already told you. The food was great."

"That's not what I'm talking about. Did the two of you get along?"

"Why not? We're both educated and professional. We discussed several new projects and other sundry items."

"What do you think of him?"

"From outward appearances, he seems withdrawn and unsure of himself. Inwardly, however, he appears to be in great pain and conflict. Of course, that's only a guess. No one really knows what's in another's brain."

"So true."

"But I have a strange sensation he's had a tremendous dilemma or crisis in the past."

Gertrude did not respond, but looked admiringly at her astute friend. "How right you are. If only you knew the pain he has endured."

Seated at the head of the huge mahogany-laminated table, Dorothy explained to the bookstore's staff, existing protocols and methodologies used by the government's task force on bugging. After finishing her prepared speech, she answered all their questions. She displayed several devices she had found in their building. "If anyone sees any of these or anything similar, please call me immediately. Whatever you do, don't touch them yourselves. They often contain an explosive detonator."

Once the lecture was finished, Gert, Austin, and Dorothy adjourned to Austin's office, Austin remarked, "You did an excellent job of explaining the monitoring concepts. I think everyone knows now what to look for, and what to do if they find anything suspicious."

"Why, thank you, Austin. I hope it helps."

"Do you expect much intervention by the Ministry now that their devices have been exposed?" Gert asked.

"Honestly, Gert, it's hard to say what they're thinking...it's a case of too many chiefs. I do believe they will try again."

"You mean bugging devices?" asked Austin.

"Perhaps, but I don't think so. I believe they will try to get us via some other means."

Austin probed farther, "Could you please give us an example of what to expect?"

"A 'for instance'? Send a box of newly published books and hope they'd still be around during an inspection."

"A setup?" asked Austin

"Exactly. It's clean and quick. Set you up for the kill and then catch you red-handed with the goods."

Gert spoke to Austin, "You'd better alert the receiving department about this possibility.

"I think I'm going to listen to Dr. Silas Barton's lecture. He's discussing *Death of A Salesman.* Anyone care to join me?"

Austin replied, "I'd love to, but Dorothy and I planned on reviewing a possible new security plan."

"Do you have any objections?" Dorothy asked Gert.

"Not at all. I'll see you at home."

Gert headed to the lecture and was surprised by the huge turnout. She found a seat at the rear of the room and listened intently as Silas masterfully discussed Miller's classic play. During the next few hours, an in-depth analysis of the book was completed by both the lecturer and his audience. Glancing at the crowd, Gert noticed a radical change. Instead of being elderly, the majority of those in attendance were either young or middle-aged. Their vitality and zest enhanced the electricity that filled the air.

"So how did you like it?" Silas asked Gert when the group had dispersed.

"Silas, it was just marvelous. I'm still amazed at some of the points you raised. I really thought I had a grasp on that book and yet, you opened my eyes to many more possibilities."

"I cannot take all the credit. I believe Miller deserves some also."

"Tell me, Silas. What do you do during the time you're not here?"

"I work at odd jobs. Since there is currently no market for a Ph.D. in English literature, and an aging college professor, I perform various tasks to support my nasty habit of living."

"Though I hate to suggest it, could you make a living by working for the government?"

"I could, but wouldn't. It simply wouldn't be the right thing to do." Gertrude was struck by the repetition of the same reason she'd heard form Donna and Edith at the party.

"How about increasing your time here? We could always use your expertise and it would give you an additional source of income."

"Thank you for the very kind offer, but I'm afraid I must decline."

"Not again," Gert muttered.

"I'm sorry, Gert. I didn't hear your question?"

"It was nothing. I was just mumbling something unimportant." Trying to change the subject, she said, "Tell me, Silas, what will you be speaking on next week?"

"I have asked a newly discovered author to come and speak about his latest book."

"Who is he or she?"

"Nathan Morrison. A gifted writer."

"Perhaps I will attend."

"I'd love for you to meet him. Some of his thoughts are just brilliant."

"By the way, have you heard how Austin's sister is feeling?"

"You mean his brother Peter, don't you? He doesn't have a sister; only one brother," Silas corrected.

"Yes. I'm mistaken. How is Peter?" Gertrude said, faking the recollection.

"The latest I heard is that he is feeling better."

Glancing at the time, Gert stated, "I'd better be going. Thanks again for the wonderful lecture."

Dorothy was pacing the floor when Gertrude arrived. "I was worried about you. I thought something terrible had happened."

"I got to talking with Silas and lost track of the time," Gert responded mildly. "He's a fascinating person. You'd be amazed what you can learn simply by asking a few questions."

"I thought you'd get caught by the curfew," mused Dorothy, still concerned.

"Tim gave me an exemption. How did your meeting go with Austin?"

"It went well. He grasps concepts quickly, and together we've come up with a good overall plan."

"I'm particularly happy to see the two of you are getting along so nicely," Gertrude observed.

Dorothy smiled, "Why not? We're both nice people."

"I haven't seen Major Whittington this week."

"He's on vacation."

"How did you know that?"

"I still have some sources left," Dorothy said slyly.

"I guess you do."

"He'll be back next week and by that time, our new system will be in place and fully functional."

FORTY-TWO

Business continued to progress smoothly. Dorothy was able to counter Major Whittington's and the government's every move. Austin and Tim administered the business despite the fact it was expanding at a rapid rate. With a staff of over ninety, the physical size of their building seemed to be constantly shrinking. To reverse this process, Gertrude successfully negotiated, and purchased the two adjacent buildings. As before, the government issued her permits quickly and without restrictions. It increased their square footage by fourfold. Lectures and discussion groups were held daily with overflowing audiences. Sales of books were never greater.

Sitting behind her new desk, Gert reviewed the architectural renderings for the new buildings with Dorothy. "What do you think?" asked Gert.

"I'm impressed. In the few short months I've been here, the business has just taken off. It appears the public is ravenous for the printed page," said Dorothy.

"It seems you are correct. I never would have believed it unless I'd seen it firsthand. I was speaking to Samuel and Rebecca, their businesses have also grown proportionately. They will require more space in our new building," Gert informed her.

"Do we have any to offer them?"

"I would never deprive them of anything. They're struggling just as we are for a cause. Weaken one leg and the horse will fall. There's strength in numbers."

"I suppose you're right. I think the Ministry would have easily closed any one of you down if you had not joined forces," Dorothy mused.

"I almost forgot to tell you some rather interesting news. I received a call yesterday from a man named Stephen Glasser. He also wants to rent space in our new building," Gertrude said.

Thinking for a moment, Dorothy inquired, "Isn't he a dealer of highly controversial material?"

"That's him. I received a follow-up letter from him in today's mail." She held up the letter. "He estimates that he requires about four hundred square feet."

"Of course, you said 'no'," Dorothy asserted.

"I did not," Gert said flatly.

"You said 'yes'? Gert, the government has been after him for years. He sells nothing but filth."

"He sells printed pages," Gert corrected her.

"You're not thinking logically at all. Have you spoken to Austin about this?"

"No. I plan on presenting it at today's meeting."

"Please don't do anything until then. Promise."

"I promise."

"We'll have the entire Ministry constantly on our backs if he is rented space in our building."

"We'll discuss it in more detail at the meeting," said Gert.

Those in attendance—besides Gert, Austin, Tim, and Dorothy—were Samuel, Rebecca, and Silas. Gertrude began, "I'd like to open today's meeting by showing you a letter we received yesterday. It's from a man who has a colossal collection of college textbooks."

"How big is big?" asked Austin.

"He states he has over 15,000 volumes," replied Gertrude.

"15,000 volumes!" exclaimed Tim.

"And they're all different," explained Gert.

"My God! I didn't know so many still existed in one place anywhere," Tim said.

"Yes, and the collection is very strong in English literature and history," Gert went on.

Silas quickly responded. "That's great. That type of book is exceedingly rare."

"Why?" inquired Dorothy.

"When Andrews assumed control of the country, one of his first edicts was to control and regulate higher education. He eliminated all existing staff and textbooks that either differed from his philosophies or were considered dangerous to his administration. Within a few short months, most college textbooks were destroyed by his troops."

"It's absolutely amazing a collection this size could have been saved," added Tim.

"I agree, and that's why we must obtain them if possible. It's a priceless commodity," Gert asserted.

Austin inquired, "What is he asking for the books?"

"The price is unimportant, but within reason."

"Great!" interjected Silas.

"I would like to vote on the matter since it means considerable work for all of us," Gertrude said. Everyone raised their hands in unanimous agreement with the purchase. Putting the letter aside, Gert concluded, "I will complete the transaction later today."

Once she received everyone's full attention again, Gertrude continued. "I received a letter from an infirm lady. She has several old and rather rare Bibles for sale. She wanted to know if we'd be interested in purchasing them. One, I believe, might be a Gutenberg."

"That's incredible!" replied Tim. "What a find!"

"Why is she selling them to us?" asked Dorothy.

"When I spoke to her today, she mentioned her terminal illness; she wants to be sure her Bibles will always be treated with respect. I promised her that service, if we decide to buy them from her. Part of the agreement is they may never be resold again. That must be incorporated into a written contract."

"What does she want for them?" Tim asked quickly.

"A reasonable amount, but only if her terms are fully agreed to."

"We've got to buy them. I can't believe it... a Gutenberg Bible..." Tim went on enthusiastically, "We'll never have this opportunity again. We have an obligation to purchase it regardless of its cost."

"Tim, what's so special about the Gutenberg Bible?" Dorothy asked.

"It was the very first book ever printed from movable type. They're exceedingly rare. I've studied and heard about them for years, but I thought Andrews destroyed them all."

Silas spoke, "I agree with Tim. We must save it for humanitarian reasons." As expected, the motion passed without opposition.

"My last letter comes from a Mr. Stephen Glasser. He wants to rent space in our building." The room exploded with opinions. "Please, one at a time." Gertrude pleaded. "Dorothy, why don't you start?"

"I'm totally against renting any space to him. He sells trash that can only hurt our image. He will attract the government to this building like fleas to a dog. We have nothing to gain and everything to lose. I'm very much opposed."

Samuel spoke next: "I've always been against the selling of such obscenities. It represents the evils of man and has been opposed for years by all decent and God-fearing people. Why waste our time talking about him? I vote against it."

Rebecca added, "Raunchy material has exploited women for years. Besides being sinful, I find it outright and flagrantly offensive. I vote no to his renting of space."

Tim then took the floor. "No, no, no...I don't want him here. There is no redeeming value to the garbage he peddles. What could we gain? I strongly vote against him."

"As do I, Gert," Austin said. "I can't believe you'd even consider the proposition. We're all doing very nicely; why rock the boat now?"

Silas stood and looked at each face. "I wholeheartedly agree with everything said so far. You each spoke the truth. His material has no literary value and in many cases, it is poorly punctuated and grossly misspelled. Exploitation of women? You're 100% correct. Each of you made a valid argument against him and yet, there are always two sides to a coin."

Gertrude smiled as Silas continued.

"You see the issue here is not whether pornography is good or bad; it's whether the government has the right to dictate what a citizen can read or cannot read. This is a vital freedom at stake. Like each one of us sitting at this table, Stephen Glasser is a crusader. He is a fighter and like all of us, he is willing to challenge the will of Andrews and the rest of his amoral government." He paused momentarily, "Whether you agree or disagree with what he sells is unimportant. What is important is that he be allowed to continue to sell whatever he wants, where he wants. This is where his struggle and our struggle converge.

"Years ago, many of our greatest classics were censored by the church, special interest groups, or by the governments themselves. Yet all have endured. Like other forms of printed literature, pornography has a specific place and will also survive. Read your Gutenberg Bible carefully, Tim, and I'm sure you will find many offensive and questionable topics. They might be considered very offensive to some and mild to others. That is what printed material is all about. Again, I ask you to reconsider your vote and think about the underlying issue of freedom of expression. The real question is censorship and the government's role in making that decision. Stephen Glasser's renting of space is secondary to the points I have raised."

Looking at each member, Silas concluded, "Despite every objection I have against pornography, I vote in favor of renting him space in the new building."

Gertrude scrutinized each face, before adding "I wholeheartedly concur with Silas. Stephen Glasser is the last of his kind; another champion of the printed page. We must help him with his fight or else he and the freedom he represents will also die...another victory for the government. By renting him space, we are adding to, and further unifying our forces. Your personal views of pornography are not consequential. What matters is the principle. I vote in favor of the motion."

When a formal vote was called a few minutes later, the proposal passed without a single negative vote. One month later, Stephen Glasser and his merchandise moved into the building. Mr. Glasser turned out to be much different than everyone had anticipated. He was articulate, stylish, and exceptionally good-looking. His friendly disposition and charming personality helped him mingle with the others who worked in the building. Everyone was astonished by the magnitude of his business; though limited to mail order, his enterprise served every region of the country.

In those first few months, whenever Gert was free from her hectic schedule, she would go to Stephen's office and visit for a few minutes. "Steve, how did you ever get into this type of business?"

Laughing and then directing his gaze upon the tiny woman, he answered, "That's a most interesting question; I'm not really sure myself."

"I was just curious about how someone, like yourself, goes into the exotic materials business?" Gert persisted.

"What you really want to know is how did I become a dealer of pornographic materials, correct?"

Smiling, she said, "I was afraid to actually say it, but how? It's an unusual choice."

143

"If you think you have a problem understanding, imagine my poor wife and daughter...trying to explain to them how I make a living."

"How do they respond?"

"When others ask, they say I am a merchandiser of provocative representations of humanistic emotions and scholarly sentiments."

"Does it usually work?" smiled Gert.

"Most people cannot fully comprehend the true meaning of the statement. They generally smile and ask another unrelated question."

"Thank goodness I haven't had to deal with that; however, owning the world's last bookstore has not prevented me from periodic ridicule, slander, and intimidation."

"I understand what you are saying; I guess it just goes with the territory."

"How did you get started?"

Feeling more relaxed, he continued. "I received my undergraduate degree from the Metropolitan College of Fine Arts."

"From MCFA? They were unequaled, probably the finest institution in the entire world for fine arts," recalled Gertrude.

"That, of course, was many years ago," confirmed Steve.

"What was your degree in?"

"Art history."

"I still don't see a connection."

"I taught at the college for several years; however, being newly married, my income was far less than needed. As a result, I was forced to supplement my earnings by working in several well-known art galleries."

"Was it exciting?"

"Yes. I got the opportunity to meet a great many artists and other dealers, but more importantly, I was able to work at what I loved the most: Art was the essence of my life."

"You mentioned your undergraduate degree. Do you also have a graduate degree?"

"Yes. I also have a degree from Uptoon College."

"Uptoon College! That's a medical school, isn't it?"

"It is."

"You mean to tell me you're a medical doctor."

"Yes I am."

"Stephen Glasser, is that really the truth?" an incredulous Gert asked.

"Yes, Gert, it is. However, if you require a physical, you'll have to see someone else. My license expired years ago."

"Steve, you're putting me on. Aren't you?"

"No, Gert. I graduated from Uptoon and practiced many years as an orthopedic surgeon."

"An orthopedist! So why are you here selling this stuff?"

"I went to medical school because of its monetary rewards and security—not for my innate love of humanity. I had little difficulty achieving these goals. Through several astute investments, my family is now financially secure for life. With that hurdle eliminated, it released me to pursue my real love once again."

"Art?"

"Yes. Through my previous contacts, a good and old friend talked me into a mail-order partnership. We specialized in the art-work of established and unknown artists."

"Did you say artwork?"

Steve raised his finger, signaling Gert to let him finish.

"Our business grew quickly and within several years, we became the largest art dealer in the country. At that point, I was torn between two successful professions."

"I guess it wasn't an easy choice."

"Not at all. Finally, after suffering from a massive case of burnout, I sold my medical practice and entered the art world on a full-time basis."

"And your wife?"

"Now that I'm no longer attempting to pursue two careers at once, she's content. After selling my practice, a series of negative events occurred. Together, they altered the course of my business and future. My business partner was brutally murdered by a gang of pre-Revolutionary terrorists."

"Some of Andrews' storm troopers?"

"Yes. He was mistaken for someone else and was shot in cold blood…right in front of our office. Despite all my years of medical training, I couldn't save his life," Steve said with regret.

"That's just terrible."

"The second factor was Andrews' successful rise to power. Once in office, he radically changed the world of art. Established artists either disappeared or simply stopped painting. Leading galleries closed and every other mail-order dealer succumbed to his pressure."

"How did you survive?"

"Perhaps it was my strong financial foundation or whatever. I refused to buckle under to their pressure and somehow I survived the crisis."

"It sounds familiar."

"In the past they have tried to close me down on technicalities; however, they stopped using any strong-arm tactics. I guess Andrews feels I am no longer a threat to his administration."

"Perhaps he's just waiting for all of us to die. Then he can eliminate our businesses without any work or bloodshed. No bullets required…one freedom after another just falls from sight. But how did you get from art to pornography?" Gert asked.

"The real question is how does one distinguish between the two. As each dealer left, I just added their different specialties to my inventory. Since my license restricts me to the buying and selling of old artwork and related materials, I just call everything art. I'm just trying to protect as many freedoms as possible. Since any new artwork is strictly prohibited by law, I am the last hope for many."

"That's quite a burden…"

"I agree, but if I give up, then the entire world of visual art has lost."

"I understand your sentiments completely and can tell you they are also shared by others within this building."

"So, whether you call my merchandise filth, porno, trash, or smut really doesn't matter. Whether the artist is Dali, Picasso, Miro, Rembrandt, or John Doe doesn't make any difference. As long as they endure Andrews' wrath, that's what is really important." Steve looked Gert straight in the eye. "That's why I elected to come here. With you and the others, I'm no longer a solitary warrior."

Touching his hand, she replied, "I guess we're all in this fight together."

"So you don't mind me selling my pornography?" Steve asked.

"Excuse me, Dr. Stephen Glasser; I rented space to the world's largest and best mail-order art dealer," Gertrude replied.

FORTY-THREE

Rebecca and Samuel listened to the morning news. The one radio station was governmentally owned and operated; with no alternative, the masses grudgingly listened to keep abreast of the latest events. "A violent storm rocked our western coast last night. High winds and heavy rains did extensive damage despite forecasting by our government's meteorological experts. Government troops have been sent by our Royal Head Commander Andrews to assist local authorities with the clean up."

Another broadcaster continued, "Royal Head Commander Andrews surprised a group of local high school students by attending their graduation ceremonies. Our eighty-three-year-old monarch and supreme leader delivered an impromptu speech for over an hour. Waving to the zealous crowd, he then left for another meeting.

"Our great leader is an amazing person," continued the broadcast. "Royal Head Commander Andrews has declared that every worker party member shall receive a twelve percent bonus in their next paycheck. Our distinguished leader is doing this in honor of our country's forthcoming Liberation Day Celebration. Naturally, he will deliver our State of the Nation address on that majestic day. We will carry it live for those of you who are unable to personally attend the ceremonies."

"Do you have any idea what our great leader will say?" asked the announcer of his colleague.

"There is some speculation, Sandy, that our Royal Head Commander Andrews will publicly outline his next ten-year plan."

"That's just sensational, Thomas. I'm sure our listeners can't wait to hear his speech."

Banging his fist on the nearest wall, Samuel shouted, "For God's sake, Rebecca, turn off that radio!"

"Please, Sam. Try to control yourself."

"Control myself? That's a joke. I'm sick and tired of hearing about our celebrated Andrews. He's everywhere!" He paced around her office. "I wake up to his name, I hear his name throughout the entire day, and I hear his name before I go to sleep. He's like a fungus; he's everywhere."

"Please, Sam. Keep your voice down."

"Keep my voice down!"

"Yes. What if the inspectors are here. We don't want anyone to hear what you're saying."

"This is no way to live. I'm sick and tired of the whole thing."

"I know...I know how you feel."

"What about us common folk? What about us?" Sam rampaged on.

Instead of answering his question, she placed her hand upon his shoulder. "It'll do no one any good if you get yourself all upset. For now, please try to calm down."

He spoke in a lower tone, "It's just so frustrating at times. We fight and fight; I wonder if it's really worth all the effort?"

"I know you really don't mean that. We'll continue to fight until the battle has been won."

"I just wish I could see even the slightest glimmer of sunshine. Something...anything."

"To be alive and remain in business throughout this period is sunshine enough. We will survive and fight a little more each day. Remember, the war is not over until the last competitor has been beaten," Rebecca reminded him.

FORTY-FOUR

During her daily routine, Gertrude strolled through the multi-building complex. Along the way, it was not unusual for her to stop and fraternize with her many employees. Despite the fact their numbers now totaled over one hundred, she made a concerted effort to know each and every one by name. "Like one big happy family," she would lecture her supervisors. "Treat them with respect and you'll receive it in return."

Stopping by Dorothy's fashionable new office, Gert stuck her head in the doorway. "Hey, lady, what are you doing?"

"Come on in, Gert. I want to show you something."

Examining various devices on the desk, Gert asked, "What are they?"

Dorothy grinned. "They're the most up-to-date government surveillance instruments."

"How did you get them?"

"I have friends in the right places."

"You've got to be kidding; I thought the past was dead."

"One should never burn all their bridges behind them. Several of my oldest friends, from my government training school years, heard of my termination. Needless to say, they were not happy about the circumstances. In fact, I'd say they were angry."

"When and how did you get a chance to speak to them?"

"There are always ways...after all, the government did train all of us to be deceptive and devious."

Gert picked up the nearest apparatus. "Where are they used?"

"Any place the government requires high surveillance . These are extremely sophisticated models."

"Would they be used against us?"

"Probably, that's why they're here. I've got to examine them closely and discover how they work."

"Aren't your friends taking a tremendous risk, giving these to you?"

"They would probably either be shot or get life in prison."

"Is it worth the risk?"

"I believe so—and so do they. They realize what happened to me could possibly happen to them."

"Is this sort of thing usual or unusual?"

"It's occurring much more frequently than ever before. I never would have considered doing such a thing, but of course, none of my friends was ever terminated. Such a tactic only weakens the morale of the Ministry's employees."

"Have you heard anything from your parents?" asked Gert cautiously.

"Not a single word. Evidently, I've been officially banned from their lives forever. I did, however, hear they are now being closely watched at all times by the Internal Security Task force." Glancing at her watch, Gert said, "I'll let you get back to your work; see you tonight at home."

"About tonight..."

"Yes. What about it?"

"Austin asked me out for dinner. Would you have any objection if I went with him?"

"Not at all."

"Are you positive? I hate leaving you alone."

"Stop worrying and just go." Gert inquired, "And where is he taking you?"

"Dinner at Franny's and then to a movie."

"A movie? I thought they were illegal?"

"They are, but this is a specially produced government movie. It's shown to the public only on rare occasions. It's a propaganda type of film generally shown to new employees or for the rehabilitation of social misfits."

"Why would you want to see that?"

"I don't. Austin wants to see it."

"Why?"

"Don't ask me. I'm just going along for a free meal. By the way, Gert, did you speak to Samuel today?"

"No. I was very busy and didn't get a chance. Is everything okay?"

"He received several recently printed newspapers in today's mail."

"New?"

"Brand new. The print was practically still wet."

"What did he do?"

"He immediately called me. I, in turn, phoned the Ministry's hot line and reported the incident."

"What did they say?"

"Only that Major Whittington was already on his way over to see us and that we should give the papers to him."

"Already on his way over?"

"Quite a coincidence, wasn't it? Anyhow he arrived within a short period and went directly to Sam's office."

"He never did that before. He always inspects Sam's area last...so what happened?"

"As he entered the doorway, we promptly handed him the package."

"Was there a problem?"

"No. I had already filled out the necessary forms and had them ready when he arrived. Between the call and the completed paperwork, there was nothing he could do."

"Any idea who sent them?"

"The package had no return address and came with a plain, brown covering."

"Postmark?"

"Smeared."

"Do you think it was a setup?"

"What else?"

"I guess we were pretty lucky."

"Lucky? I'd say more like good planning and solid security."

"How is Sam?"

"Slightly shaken up, but glad it ended the way it did."

"Maybe I should go upstairs and see how he's doing?"

"Rebecca drove him home earlier. She was concerned about his health."

"What's wrong with his health?"

"He has a history of a heart problem. Didn't he ever tell you?"

"No."

"Anyway, don't worry; Sam's wife called a short time ago and said he is feeling much better."

"What about his business?"

"Tim will cover for him while he's gone. It's all arranged. He only expects to be out for a few days."

"I'd better be going and let you get back to your work." Grinning, Gert added, "I'll see you tonight when you get home—and enjoy your date."

Gertrude resumed her walk. When she reached the employees' lounge, she studied the activities bulletin board on the far wall.

"Anything interesting, Miss Johnson?" a janitor named Mark ventured.

"They're all of interest to me, Mark."

"I know exactly what you mean, Miss Johnson. That's why I

love working here. The extras are just the greatest."

"Thank you. I consider that a pleasant compliment."

"I meant it. By the way, did you go to the lecture given by Nathan Morrison?"

"Did I! I thought it was sensational."

"I agree. He impressed everyone, including Silas."

"It's too bad he didn't live long ago instead of now."

"Why?"

"Then we would have his thoughts in print," observed Mark.

"I see your point," said Gertrude, impressed. "With his radical views and controversial ideas, I'm sure the government would like to see him quickly fade into the woodwork."

"I'm afraid I don't get involved in politics, Miss Johnson; I'm just a plain old floor sweeper."

"There's nothing wrong with that, Mark. In fact, you're the best one we have in the entire building."

"Thank you, Miss Johnson." Blushing slightly, he continued, "I'd better get going; I've got a lot more cleaning to do before my shift is over."

Gertrude continued her walk. As she reached the basement, she scanned the huge warehouse and storage area. Shelves and boxes of books filled the entire room. The sight always seemed to inspire her...from one small shop to this.

Along an isolated corridor, she observed a large pile of debris against one wall. Instead of walking past the sector, she stopped and investigated the accumulation of rubbish. Not recalling its presence during any of her previous jaunts, she pushed aside several of the cartons. Worried about a potential fire hazard, she tried to determine why it was there in the first place.

The removal of several additional boxes exposed a hidden door. Why block a doorway? Not only doesn't it make any sense, but it's also illegal. Turning the knob, she discovered it was locked. Since no other internal doors were ever locked, Gertrude placed her master key into the deadbolt, but found it did not fit. "What's going on here?" she spoke softly to herself. Hastily walking to the nearest wall phone, she paged Mark. "Please come down here immediately. I'm in the hallway with the pile of boxes."

"I know exactly where you are; I'll be right down."

"Bring your master key with you. Something is wrong with mine." He arrived minutes later.

Gasping for breath, he said, "I ran all the way, Miss Johnson. How can I help you?"

"Who left these boxes here?"

"I did, Miss Johnson."

"Why did you do it? It's against the law."

"I didn't know that, but it doesn't matter anyhow. I was ordered to put them there."

"By who?"

"Mr. Mathews. He told me always to keep things piled in front of this door."

"Austin?"

"Yes, Miss Johnson—and he reminds me about it all the time."

"I'll have to speak with him about it. Anyway, please give me your master key for a minute." He handed her his key and watched as she unsuccessfully tried to unlock the door. "Who has the key for this room?"

"I believe Mr. Mathews has the only one."

"Why?"

"I have no idea, Miss Johnson. I'm only a sweeper, it wouldn't be right for me to question my bosses."

"That's true. Please forgive my impatience. Do you know where Mr. Mathews keeps the key?"

"I saw it once in the top drawer of his desk. It had a green label, but please don't tell him I told you."

"I won't." Looking once more at the door, she replied, "Thank you, Mark, you can go back to your work." She headed directly to Austin's office and finding he had left for the day, she opened his top desk drawer. There, in the far corner, was the key. She returned to the mysterious door. Placing it into the lock's cylinder, she nervously turned it. One click and it opened. Pushing it inward, she peeked into the darkened room. She found a light switch by running her hand along the wall. Instantly, three lights illuminated the area.

Inching her way into the box-filled room, she surveyed the contents. *What's so special? Why is it locked?* Studying a nearby sealed carton, nothing abnormal could be detected. Taking her small penknife, she cut along the top seam of one of the boxes. Pushing aside the flap, she gazed at the contents. "No!" she screamed. "No!"

Picking up a book, she stared at each letter engraved on the cover. Her shrieks reverberated throughout the small room and hallway. For the longest period, she remained stationary and gaped at the many cartons. "Why?" Gertrude's disillusioned voice trembled. Finally, she took the book with her, turned off the lights, and relocked the door. After returning Austin's key, she sought refuge in the privacy of her office. Placing the book on the top of her desk, she sat heavily in her chair and continued to stare. *What do I do now?* For the rest of the night, Gert stared at the newly published copy of Nathan Morrison's, *In Quest of Justice and Freedom.*

The second the morning curfew ended, Dorothy drove to the bookstore. After parking the car, she bolted across the street. Breathless, she managed to unlock the front door. "Gert, are you here?" she screamed. Hearing no response, she raced up the flight of stairs toward the office at the end of the hallway. "Gert, are you here?" She shouted again as she flung open the door.

Finding her friend sitting silently behind her large desk, Dorothy ran to her side. With tears flowing freely down her cheeks, Dorothy cried, "Oh, Gert, thank goodness you're alive! I was so worried." Tenderly stroking the elderly woman's arms she babbled, "I was so frightened. Thank goodness you're okay. I was so worried."

Gertrude slowly lifted her hand and affectionately touched the younger woman's cheek. She wiped away several tears and softly whispered, "I'm okay, please don't cry."

"Oh, Gert, what happened? I didn't sleep the whole night. I was afraid something happened to you." She tried to control her emotional outburst. "When I came home last night and found you weren't there, I panicked. All I could think about was being alone again." She cried, "I was so worried, so worried."

Embracing her friend, Gertrude whispered, "I'm just fine. Just relax."

After several minutes, Dorothy sat on the floor at her friend's feet. With her head resting on Gert's lap, she asked, "Why didn't you come home last night?"

"I had some important work to catch up on."

"Why didn't you bring it home?"

"I got so wrapped up in my work I literally forgot the time. Before I knew what was happening, the curfew was in effect. Not having a pass, I decided to finish what I was doing and sleep here."

"But I called and called."

"I slept in the employees' lounge. I guess I just didn't hear the phone ringing. I'm so sorry I caused you to worry."

"It's okay as long as you're safe. That's all that matters." Hugging Gert's legs and half laughing, she sobbed, "You certainly gave me a dreadful fright and a night without any sleep." Looking up she pleaded, "Please don't do it again. I don't think my heart can take it."

Kissing the top of her head, Gertrude consoled, "I'm sorry."

"Aren't you going to ask me about last night?"

"What about it?"

"Don't you remember? I had a date with Austin."

"Austin...oh yes, I forgot about it."

"Gert, are you sure you're feeling okay?"

"I told you I am fine. Why do you ask?"

"No reason. Anyhow, Austin and I had a marvelous time. I

really think he's quite warm and tender once you break through his facade. It's a good thing, however, I'm not jealous because all he talked about was you. Are you surprised?"

"Oh...that's nice," remarked Gertrude flatly.

"Gert, you didn't hear a single word I said, did you?"

"I guess I was daydreaming. Could you repeat it?"

Giggling and crying at the same time, Dorothy responded, "It's not important. I'll tell you about it some other time. I'm just so happy you're alive and healthy." They spoke for another half hour before Dorothy stood. "I'd better get to work. I think Major Whittington might be inspecting us today."

"Intuition?"

"No. Inside information, but don't worry, all our paperwork is already completed."

"I never worry about things like that." They hugged each other and Dorothy left.

Gert got up, locked the door, and removed Morrison's book from her desk. She again began to contemplate her options. The buzzing of her intercom disturbed her concentration. "Yes, Mary. What is it?"

"Miss Johnson, I just wanted to remind you about your meeting with Austin and Tim in fifteen minutes."

"Call them and tell them I won't be there."

"Yes, Miss Johnson. Shall I reschedule another?"

"Absolutely not. Just tell them I'm very busy."

"I will do it immediately."

"And hold all my calls. I don't want to speak to or see anyone other than Dorothy. Is that clear?"

"Yes, Miss Johnson. Will there be anything else?"

"Yes. Don't disturb me any more today. I have a lot of important things to do." After hanging up the receiver, Gert leaned back in her chair and stared at the book. *Now what?*

FORTY-FIVE

Several nights later, Gertrude was preparing for bed.

"May I speak to you for a minute?" Dorothy said from the doorway.

"Certainly, Dorothy, come in."

"I'm still concerned about you. For the last few days, you've been acting differently."

"I know. I have a great many things on my mind."

"Anything you want to talk about with a friend?"

"No. It's something I've got to work out by myself."

"I know how you feel; everyone goes through these times sometime during their lives. It's actually quite normal."

"You mean I'm human after all?"

Dorothy gave Gert a tender embrace. "Yes you are, and I love you very much."

"I love you, too."

"I have a small favor to ask," Dorothy began.

"Just name it and it's yours."

"Austin is exceedingly upset. You haven't spoken to him or seen him in days. He has called your office many times and has been told you are too busy to speak to him and yet, you always talk to me. Could you please call him tomorrow and calm him down? I hate to see him this way."

"No."

Dorothy was shocked. "No?"

"You heard what I said. Just plain no!"

"Nothing more? Without an explanation to either of us? Don't you think we both deserve more than that?"

"No. When I'm ready to talk to him, I will."

"Gert, I don't think that's very fair. Austin's always been there for you."

"I'd rather not discuss this subject any further. I'll speak to him when I'm good and ready. Not one minute before." Seeing she was getting nowhere, Dorothy returned to her room.

The next morning neither spoke on the way to work. After parking the car, Dorothy turned to her friend. "Please, Gert, he's taking it so badly. I don't understand how you could do this to another human being. You're not being fair to him at all. For my sake, would you please talk to him?"

"I'll speak to him when I'm ready to do so and not a second sooner," Gert repeated.

The next morning, Gert pressed her intercom. "Mary."

Answering in an apprehensive tone, Mary said, "Miss Johnson, is that you?"

"Please tell Dr. Austin Mathews I would like to see him in my office immediately."

"Yes, Miss Johnson. Is there anything else that—"

"Mary!"

Yes, Miss Johnson."

"Please tell Dr. Mathews to come." Five minutes later, a knock sounded at her door. "Come in."

Austin entered with a large smile. "Thank you for seeing me, Gert; I was afraid—"

"Dr. Mathews, a recent situation has been brought to my attention. It has caused me a great deal of personal anguish."

"Can I help in any way?"

"I'm sure you can, Dr. Mathews, but let me explain a few more things." Staring him straight in the face, Gert continued, "Last week I found this." Taking Morrison's book from the drawer, she placed it on her desk top. "I demand an explanation and while we're on the subject, Dr. Mathews, I believe I'm entitled to some other clarifications. Why have you lied to me continually about certain facts?" She leaned forward and said, "Dr. Mathews, I may be old, but I'm far from being blind or stupid."

He meekly sat and stared at the book while she continued her tirade: "An educated man—if you really are one—should be able to come up with something. After all, you've been putting on a great act so far. Come on, Dr. Mathews, where's your smooth-talking tongue now?"

"Where did you find it?" he all but whispered.

"That is none of your business nor is it any of your concern. I just want to know why you've used me all this time? Several times you actually had me fooled. Was I stupid?" Standing, she continued. "I demand an explanation. You've hurt me deeply, but I won't let you hurt my Dorothy. It would just kill her if she ever found out what kind of person you really are." She took a second to catch her breath. "You're not a lowlife, you're much worse. I cannot find the words to describe my disappointment and pain."

Finally Austin spoke, "You have every right in the world to feel the way you do; I'd probably draw the same conclusions if I were in your position. Unfortunately, however, everything is not quite as simple or accurate as it appears. I am going to tell you the truth. You may not like what you hear, but you do deserve an explanation.

"Have you ever heard of PAT?"

"PAT?" repeated Gert.

"It is an organization formed years ago by several leading educators."

"What type of organization?"

"PAT stands for People Against Tyranny."

"Without appearing stupid, I'm afraid I can't make the connection."

"We have dedicated our lives to fight our government's persecution and restore human rights."

"That is very noble of you, but how do you explain the book in my building?"

"Perhaps seeing is better than my trying to explain our ideologies and philosophies. I would like to take you to our headquarters."

"Why should I go anywhere with you? You've lied to me constantly."

"Not about everything, Gert. Please come and see for yourself."

"You mean you've actually told the truth once in awhile?"

"Please. I beg you to see it," Austin pleaded.

After a long moment of deliberation, Gert picked up the phone. "Hello, Dorothy, this is Gert. I'm not sure what time I'll be home, so don't worry about me."

"Is everything okay? Are you ill and not telling me the truth?"

"I'm just fine. I'm going out with Austin and we're not sure when we'll be returning. I just didn't want you to worry unnecessarily."

"With Austin? I'm so glad. Is everything back to normal between the two of you again?"

"I can't discuss it now; I'll have a lot to tell you when I see you later." After hanging up, she donned her coat and grabbed her pocketbook. "Dr. Mathews, I'm ready to see your PAT, but I want you to know it is your last chance." He stood and turned for the doorway. "Did you forget something?" asked Gert.

Looking around, he answered, "I don't see...."

"Take that book with you and I never want to see it in my building ever again. I expect you to dispose of all of them by the end of today. Do I make myself clear?"

F O R T Y - S I X

The car picked its way through city streets and finally into the neighboring countryside. Gertrude gazed out the window as the concrete jungle slowly gave way to trees and other greenery. Neither said a single word nor looked at one another. After nearly two hours of driving, Austin steered the car off the main highway. Fifteen minutes later, he drove onto a bumpy side road. Gert looked at the underbrush and nearby fields and realized she had no idea where they were. Austin, the man whom she had once fully trusted, was now an unfamiliar stranger.

At the end of the dirt road, the car came to an abrupt halt. "Please stay here; I'll be back." He exited and quickly disappeared into the woods. After ten minutes of waiting, she opened the door and stood alongside the vehicle. She studied the area for any clues, but nothing could be detected. All she could see was a deep thicket of trees and shrubs.

The sound of footsteps startled her. Austin emerged from the woods. "It's clear to proceed."

"I was wondering if you'd decided to just leave me here."

"Please, Gert. You'll get your answers soon. Follow me closely and don't step off the path at any time. They walked silently through the woods. Austin constantly surveyed the region as if expecting someone or something to become visible. "Would you like to stop and rest for a few minutes?" he asked.

"No, Dr. Mathews, I am just fine. Let's just get this over with. I've got a lot of work to do at my store." The terrain was getting rougher, but despite her advanced age, she had no difficulty in keeping up with the younger man. She attempted to memorize their trek, but a complexity of paths soon made it an impossible task. As they reached the end of the forest, Austin stopped. "Wait here." He moved forward, brought his hands to his mouth, then proceeded to shout three piercing cries. Moments later, three similar cries replied. "It is now safe to continue." Gert had a multitude of questions, but remained silent and followed him along the path. After a short time, he stopped and pointed ahead. "Here we are."

"Where? I don't see anything."

"Beyond that huge boulder. Do you see the cave? That's our destination."

"A cave?"

"Yes, Gert. In that cave lies all the answers you seek." Nearing the giant portal, Austin slowed his pace. "Be careful. There's loose debris on the ground." Locating two flashlights conveniently placed along the wall, Austin handed one to her. She hesitated for a second, then followed him into the darkness. Rounding a small bend, they came upon a large, wooden doorway.

Austin knocked loudly three times and then repeated his three verbal shouts. The door opened and a man appeared from the darkness. As their light found its way to his face, Gertrude stepped backward in shock. "Silas!"

"Welcome to PAT."

Positioned between Silas and Austin, Gertrude stared in astonishment at those seated around the table: Every last person was a member of her staff. Finally, Silas broke the silence. "Many years ago, Andrews' storm troopers ravaged the country. Several other uncompromising educators and I secretly vowed to resist and confront the catastrophic epidemic with every ounce of strength we could muster. Instead of turning the other cheek, we established an underground resistance movement. It was appropriately named People Against Tyranny or PAT for short."

He continued: "Our goals are to preserve the printed page and to protect the individual rights of our citizenry. The task has been exceptionally arduous. Dedicated members have been either jailed or killed along the way. Despite personal sacrifices—and there have been a great many—we continue to strive for our original objectives. Unlike yourself who has a license, we cannot fight openly; we must work under a cloak of perpetual secrecy. We use whatever means are available at the time to right the wrong that haunts our society. It has been a long and unyielding path we have selected, but none of us will ever give up the fight." He looked at Gertrude with great affection and kinship. "I'm sure you must have many questions at this point. Please feel free to ask them."

"This is like a nightmare... I can't believe it is actually real." Looking around, she asked, "Is everyone at my store a member of PAT?"

"Everyone except you, Samuel, Rebecca, Stephen, and the custodial staff."

"Dorothy also?"

"Of course not; she was government."

"How long have you been in my store?"

"Ever since Austin's employment. From there, as your business grew—with our help I might add—additional members were added to your staff."

"What about Tim?"

"He's supervising your store right now, but he's also with us."

"What about Sam's, Rebecca's, and Stephen's staff?"

"Also our members."

"Why did you choose to infiltrate us?"

"The four of you represent, in a way, our last link with the outside world. You're like our bridge to the citizens of our country. Since we cannot deal directly with them, we have selected the four of you to act as our representatives."

"Do any of them know?"

"Not at all. We've managed to remain well hidden this entire time."

"Why not come out in the open with your cause?"

"It would be sheer suicide at this time. Andrews would crush us before we even got started. He's much too strong and we're much too weak. Besides, the public isn't quite ready for a change."

"I suppose you're right," Gert conceded.

Silas continued, "Gert, each of us is willing to give up our lives for PAT's convictions. We've been agonizing for years; if you and the others fail, I'm afraid PAT will also deteriorate. In a way your businesses and our organization are interdependent for survival."

"Austin, why didn't you mention any of this to me before?" accused Gert.

"I was afraid you wouldn't believe any of it."

"You're probably correct.... By the way, do you really have a sister?"

"No. I only have a brother named Peter."

"And Tim's parents?"

"Both dead."

"Why did you lie to me about those things?"

"What would have been your reaction if I told you the truth?"

"I see your point." Turning towards Silas, Gert asked, "Silas?"

"Yes?"

"Are you really a Ph.D.?"

"Yes, that is true."

"What about Austin and Tim?"

"Both were my students and have doctoral degrees in English literature."

"And my other staff members?"

"Everyone has either a Masters or Ph.D. degree in English literature or some related subject."

"That explains a great many things. Why are you here in this location?"

"It's safe yet convenient to the city."

"How do you plan on fighting Andrews?"

"Through a great amount of work, fortitude, and patience."

"It sounds like an impossible task."

"What about you, Gert?"

"What about me?"

"How do you manage to keep Andrews and the government at bay and from closing you down?"

"Well, you of all people know: hard work and meticulous planning."

"Precisely our strategy."

"Have you ever infiltrated other bookstores or businesses in the past?"

"As many as we could."

"Schneiders?"

"Of course. Roy and I were good friends. We could have achieved many good things together, but unfortunately, he was murdered by Andrews' storm troopers."

"What do you want from me?"

"Your support and cooperation."

"Why should I? I've been lied to so many times I won't know what's fact or fiction."

"Because neither one of us can survive without the other."

"Perhaps. I believe I'd like to think about it."

"I concur. I'm sure this whole thing has been quite a shock to your system," Silas said affectionately.

"It certainly has been," Gert replied.

"Would you like to rest before we continue?"

"Continue?"

"Yes, there is much more to see and discuss."

"I've got to get back to my store," she objected.

"Austin has already notified Dorothy you'll be staying at his house for a few days and Tim will run the store. Everything has been arranged."

"But—"

"Please give us a chance to adequately present our case. That's all we ask. Give us a little more time."

Looking at each familiar face at the table, she finally answered, "Okay, I agree."

"Excellent. Austin will take you to your room and care for your needs. I'll see you again in the morning."

"Silas?"

"Yes, Gert."

"Is this as dangerous as I think?"

"More so, but to win would make all the sacrifices and hardships worthwhile." Rising from his chair Silas said, "We'll continue the discussion in the morning."

F O R T Y - S E V E N

"Where is Austin?" Gertrude asked Silas.

"He went back to the store. You'll be my guest for the next few days."

"I really can't. I must be getting back."

"I'm afraid that's impossible. The car will not be returning until Friday."

Gert was frustrated and slightly angered by his answer. Silas ignored her reaction.

"I thought I'd start by taking you to our writing room."

"What's a writing room?"

"You will see soon enough. Please follow me."

They spoke along the way about the founders of PAT and its origins. "So you are the last of the originators?" queried Gertrude.

"That is correct." Opening another wooden door, Gertrude was pleasantly surprised and impressed by the room's interior. It was brilliantly colored and appeared to be professionally decorated. The far left wall was shelved and completely filled with books. "That is the smaller of our two reference libraries."

"It appears to be quite complete."

"It's usually adequate; however, those of us requiring additional information must use our other library."

"I'd like to see it before I leave if possible."

"You've already seen it."

"I'm sorry, I can't remember."

"It's not here...it's your bookstore." They were interrupted by another voice.

"Hello, Miss Johnson, I'm glad you decided to come. Welcome to PAT."

"Nathan Morrison, what are you doing here?"

"Doing here? This is my whole life. Without Silas and the others, I wouldn't have gotten as far as I have."

"I'm afraid I must leave you two for the remainder of the day. I have a rather pressing matter that must be cared for immediately," Silas said abruptly and left.

After he had gone, Gert asked, "What do you want to show me, Nathan?"

"To truly appreciate a completed book, I'd like you to spend time with me and the others who work in this section. Have you ever written anything?"

"No. I do not have the patience or the talent."

"Nearly everyone has the potential to write, it's simply a matter of hard work and developing one's individual skills. For instance, my last book was titled *In Quest of Justice and Freedom*."

"That's the one I found at my store."

"Have you read it?"

"No. Let's just say I've seen it quite a bit lately."

"The first draft took over four years to write."

"Four years?...but it wasn't that long."

"That was with the assistance of my friends here."

"How many writers work here?"

"Fifteen are on site and at least one hundred more are in the field."

"In the field? Where?"

"Scattered throughout the breadth of the country. When a novel is finished by the author, they get it to us for our evaluation. Once approved, it is published."

"I thought—"

"We'll go into that end later. Right now, I'd like you to join us in assessing a recently submitted book." They walked over to a huge circle of the other full-time authors and together they dissected the manuscript. After each member expressed their opinion, Gert was asked to comment.

"It was good; however, the story line resembles one already written years ago," she surmised.

"Which one?"

"It was called *The Metamorphoses*, by Franz Kafka." Feeling more at ease, she continued. "Kafka utilized a similar theme but he used a cockroach, whereas this author uses a mouse. Their text was very similar, if not identical."

"Do you have a copy of the book in your store?"

"I believe so."

"We'll send her back her manuscript next week. With it, we'll include our critique and—with your permission, Gert—a copy of Kafka's book." Everyone agreed. They then assessed three additional submissions. Gert added terrific insight to each discussion. Only one was found to be original in content and worthy of any future consideration.

After the meeting, she joined Ted Putter at his desk. He explained how he began each of his books and the research involved in formulating a central theme or character. Throughout this time, she questioned him thoroughly. They were later rejoined by Nathan Morrison. "Miss Johnson, you could be a great help to us," Nathan remarked.

"How? I'm not a writer."

You're very gifted—and quite talented in other ways. Your expertise with the printed page is far beyond any of us. I'd say you're equal to Dr. Barton."

"Thank you, but I doubt all of that. I still don't see how I could be of any help."

"You saved us a great deal of time by your knowledge of books and authors...and your ability to analyze plots, themes, and characters is uncanny. Perhaps it's because of your tremendous interest in books, or an innate quality that simply exists. Regardless, it's there and we'd love to be able to capitalize on it when necessary."

"I'm not sure I agree with your assessment..."

"We look myopically at each book; we scrutinize and criticize as editors. We're concerned about periods, commas, etc. You analyze the same book in a more subjective, global manner. It's both refreshing and complimentary to our methodologies."

"A gestalt approach..." Gert responded.

"Exactly. I would like to suggest that others also utilize your skills as needed; you could be a valuable source."

"I can't come here."

"Understood. And we would not take advantage of or abuse your time in any way. What if we sent you a brief summary of any book being considered for publication? Would you comment on its plot and story theme?"

"I don't see why not; that won't take me too much time," Gert agreed.

"If a book is already the same or similar to one already printed, we'll purchase the copy from you and send it to the author of the manuscript."

"Why go through all of this? Why not just publish them?"

"We have a very limited capacity for manufacturing and distribution, so we have no choice but to be extremely selective. Though we'd like to accept every submission, we can't do it from a practical standpoint."

"How many actually get published?"

"We try to print sixty to seventy-five books a year."

"How are they distributed?"

"That is not our department; others are responsible for that task."

The rest of the day was spent equally among the other writers. Though each varied in technique and style, Gertrude was soon impressed with their individual adoration of, and devotion to their work.

At dinner, she sat with Silas who asked, "How did you find your day?"

"I learned quite a lot. I'd only seen the end product of publishing prior to today and this experience has opened my eyes to a great many things. It was intriguing to meet the creators of such works. They are so very gifted. How did you find them?"

"They find us. Unfortunately we can only accommodate a select few as there are many more on a waiting list, all of whom are just as bright, talented, and creative. We've been discussing the possibility of establishing another center elsewhere, but it has been put on hold."

"Why?"

"Other matters of greater import have recently come up."

Not wanting to pry, she changed topics. "Does anyone draw a salary?"

"No. All monies from our publishing division help sustain the organization. That is one of the reasons why your bookstore is so vital to our very existence. It not only provides reference materials for research, but it permits all the members of our departments to mingle on a regular basis. Another important reason is that each member can earn enough money to survive in a real, capitalistic world."

"Including you?"

"My demands are few. My goal is not the accumulation of wealth or power. I am content with my present situation."

"Are these the odd jobs everyone has spoken about?"

Chuckling. "Yes. Working for PAT is our 'odd jobs.' In reality, however, being employed at your store is the secondary issue."

"Do you or the other members ever sleep?"

"Not very much. Each of us manages to get a few hours a night. That's, of course, if we're lucky."

"How do you do it?"

"I really don't know myself, but no one has complained lately.

Either we're all plain stupid or terribly dedicated. I prefer to think we're dedicated."

"I'm concerned about Dorothy."

"She's fine. Austin is keeping a close watch on her."

"And my store?"

"We had another inspection today, but we passed without any difficulty."

"Silas, I have one last question to ask: Can either of us really win?"

Without hesitation he replied, "We don't have a choice; we must."

"Gertrude Johnson, I'd like you to meet our head production editor, Bryan Feld," Silas pronounced the next morning.

"It's a pleasure to meet you."

"Likewise."

"You will spend the day with Bryan. He will enlighten you about another aspect of our operation."

Once Silas left the room, Bryan showed Gertrude their physical plant. "This is where we actually print the final product. All our presses and equipment are located here."

"It's quite impressive."

"I agree, but there is a great deal of work before a book actually gets this far." He took her to his office. "I or the other production editors must take the author's raw manuscript and transform it into a completed book. Many different steps are included within this process."

Feeling at ease, Gert asked, "How is it done?"

"I'll briefly outline a typical scenario. Once a raw manuscript is approved for publication by our in-house staff, it is given to one of our department's production editors. We very carefully recheck all their work. Of course we are not concerned with the actual content or story line, but rather with the raw mechanics."

"Could you be more specific?"

"Yes. We look at spelling, grammar, and punctuation."

"What are the qualifications of your editors?"

"Each one has a Ph.D. in English."

"Like Silas?"

"Precisely, except that Silas has two doctorates. The second one is in psychology."

"He never told me."

"Silas is a man of few words; he obtains respect by his wisdom and deeds."

"Does he have a family?"

"No. He has devoted his entire life to PAT."

Gert shook her head slowly and attempted to fully comprehend Silas' dedication. "He's unbelievable."

"That's true and that's why PAT is still operative. He has been a role model for all of us to respect and follow. We must, however, discuss other topics at this time."

"I'm sorry; please continue."

"Once we recheck the manuscript, it is given to one of our type-setters. At that time, we provide them with our exact specifications. They perform their work and send us back galleys. They then must be rechecked to make sure they are perfect."

"Sounds like a lot of rechecking."

"Lots. Pages are then reset and returned to the typesetter for any changes. Once approved, a camera copy is presented to our editors."

"And then the book?"

"Not yet. The printer gives a set of book blues to the editor. After one last inspection, and if approved, the book is finally printed. Collating, binding, and other concluding tasks are completed then."

"All this work is done here?"

"Yes We have the capability to produce all types of books; how-ever, we try to keep them all of a uniform size."

"Why?"

"One of our biggest problems is the distribution of the final product to our customers. Odd-sized books can't be easily hidden or shipped."

"Where did you get all your equipment?" Gertrude asked.

"Mostly donations from printers forced out of business. They'd rather give the presses to us for nothing than have the government destroy them."

"I never realized all the work involved in producing a book," Gert observed.

"The majority of people don't. Please remember we are also perfectionists. Our books are more than mere page and print; they represent PAT."

For the remainder of the day, the staff introduced Gertrude to the fundamentals of their departments. She had little difficulty grasping the procedures, and questioned them freely about their role within the entire organization. Each member in turn, became impressed by her keen insight and analytical mind. Later that evening, she met again with Silas, who asked, "What do you think of our print shop?"

"I'm overwhelmed by both your physical plant and your staff."

"You'll leave tomorrow evening. Austin will be coming to get you."

"Good."

"I would like the privilege of spending the entire day tomorrow with you."

"I believe I'd enjoy it, Silas. Thank you." Early the next morning, they met.

"How do you feel about going outside in the sunlight?" asked Silas.

"I would enjoy it very much. I miss the fresh air," Gert replied.

"I'll arrange for a box lunch; we can have ourselves an old-fashioned picnic."

Silas spread the blanket beside a brook and helped Gertrude to sit. "Tell me, Silas. Why?"

"I owe it to them... I owe it to all those who have fallen in battle."

Gazing at the serene setting, Gert asked, "What can I do to

help? I'm an old woman just trying to keep my business together."

"You are much more, Gertrude Johnson. Much more than you can even imagine. You have become a inspirational leader to all those who know and love you. You are quickly becoming a living legend among those in the literary world."

"It's you, Silas. It is you who are the living legend. Without you, none of this could have happened."

Sighing, he continued, "There's something I must tell you."

Noticing his somber tone, she inquired, "What is it?"

Tenderly holding her hand, he said softly, "Gert, I'm dying."

Gertrude did not immediately respond. Finally regaining her composure, she asked, "Dying! My God, Silas, are you sure?"

"Positive. I have only a few more months left according to my doctors...so little time and so much to do."

"What about Austin or Tim? Do they know?"

"No. I trust you will keep it a secret."

"You have my word."

"Gert, I must pass my scepter to another, equally qualified person." Taking a deep breath, he continued, "I feel you are the most capable and best person to take my place."

"Me?" Gertrude was astounded.

"Yes."

"There are others more competent and skilled to take your place. I don't even have a college degree."

"You possess wisdom, insight, and patience. You're a natural leader among people. You speak the truth and guide from the heart. That is enough."

"How can I do it? I'm an old woman."

"Water tends to seek its own level. You will accomplish what must be achieved."

"It's not fair, Silas. I didn't ask for any of this. Why me?"

"It is your destiny and must be accepted. I am only giving you something you already possess."

"What if I don't take it from you?"

178

"Then our entire endeavor will end."

"What about Austin or Tim? They certainly know much more than me about PAT—"

"You already know the answer to the question, Gert. In your heart, you recognize the truth."

"But it's illegal. They'll close my store if we're caught."

Countering, he added, "The government will close your store as soon as you're gone anyway. You are offering a temporary remedy to an incorrigible and unacceptable situation."

"But—"

"PAT is society's only long-range chance. If we fail to meet our objectives, then our country will never again enjoy the printed page." Pausing momentarily, he pleaded, "Please think about what I have said. You know in your heart I am correct."

Gert sat silently for the longest time. Finally, she reached outward, held his hand, and sobbed. "Silas, I'm frightened."

"I understand how you must feel; just trust your instincts."

"What if the other people won't follow me or listen to what I say?"

"They will."

"I'm very confused. Why did you do this to me?"

"I'm also scared. I have fought my entire life for a cause and it appears I'll be dying before it's ever achieved. It's a very frustrating realization. You are my only hope for attaining that goal. All I ask is that you carry on my work and at least try."

"I will try," she sighed. "For you, Dr. Silas Barton, I will try."

They ate lunch and spent a leisurely afternoon together. During that time, they discussed their favorite books and other literary subjects. A distant honking disturbed their conversation. "Austin is here. It's time for you to go home."

"Silas, I've enjoyed this so much. Can't he wait a little longer?"

"No, Gert, it's time to leave."

"Can we do it again in the future? It was just delightful."

"I wish we could, but somehow I doubt if it will ever come to pass."

Gert stated, "I've never been more frightened of anything in my entire lifetime."

Leaning toward her, Silas whispered, "Gertrude Johnson, I pass my being on to you."

"I will try, Silas. I will try my very best to carry on your legacy."

As they neared the car, Austin eagerly waved to Silas. "Will you be coming back with us?"

"No. I have a lot of work. There's too little time and too much to do."

"Please take care of yourself."

"I will and Gert, please—" entreated Silas.

"I promise; you have my word on it."

Austin pulled the car onto the highway and headed towards the city. "Austin?" began Gert.

"Yes?"

"How are Dorothy and the store?"

"Both eagerly await your return."

"Good. I'm glad to be headed home." As they entered the inner city, she spoke again, "I'm sorry, Austin. I misjudged your intentions and I apologize. I just didn't know or understand."

"It's fine, Gert. No apology is necessary. By the way, did Silas mention when he was planning on giving us another lecture?"

"I believe he's going to be away from the store for awhile. I think he's working on another project." She looked at the younger man at her side. "He did request that you and Tim take over his lecturing until he returns."

"Tim and I will gladly do it for him."

"Thank you, and I'm sure Silas will be grateful." After he parked the car in their lot, Gertrude reached over and held his hand. "I will try."

"I'm afraid I don't understand what you mean," Austin said.

"Some day you will, but right now, let's go inside and see how everyone is doing."

FORTY-EIGHT

The news of Silas' death spread quickly. It had been nearly four months since Gertrude's visit to PAT's secret headquarters, but her involvement and influence upon the organization had already been felt. Weekly manuscript reviews were becoming commonplace and the flow of books sent to authors was increasing at a fantastic rate. To fully capitalize on the elderly owner's expertise and limited schedule, the key members of PAT met regularly and outlined their strategies for utilizing her services. Dorothy, at Gert's request, maintained a debugged area for these meetings. Of course, Dorothy was not permitted to attend or given access to anything discussed.

Silas had chosen to be buried in a small cemetery on the outskirts of the city as close to the cave as possible. Despite their huge volume of work, every business in the building closed to honor their friend and associate. With over four hundred persons in attendance, Austin delivered a touching eulogy. Tears flowed as the educator's casket was lowered into the cold earth. As each person left, they dropped a rose into the freshly dug hole. Little was said for the remainder of the day as individual groups met in solace. Everyone mourned and missed their deceased mentor.

Early the next morning, Gert met with Austin, Tim, Nathan, and Bryan. Tim was the first to address the group. "Before Silas died, he left each of us sealed envelopes. We were told not to open any of them until the day after his funeral." Handing an envelope to Gert, he stated, "This one is for you." Once the distribution was completed, he said, "I have been instructed by Silas to ask Austin to open his first."

Austin opened it and read the note aloud: "The time for grieving should always be short. Give her your full support and devotion."

Tim read his letter next: "Inexperience is a positive factor. It permits clear and objective thought. Don't be deceived by age or facade."

Nathan was next: "And it shall come to pass that a new leader will emerge and she will lead her troops to victory. Tyranny will falter in her path."

Bryan was the next to open his envelope: "A leader cannot stand alone, she must have the endorsement of everyone involved. If she falters and falls, all will be forever lost."

Everyone gazed at Gertrude. With shaking hands, she held the handwritten letter. She read it silently and allowed it to drop to the table. Austin picked it up and read it aloud: "My scepter is now passed to you. Think as many, and always remember our goals. We are now united. Love, Silas."

Gertrude wanted to respond, but she remained mute. Sensing her uneasiness, Austin addressed the group. "It appears Silas has given us his legacy. I believe his judgment is correct. Does anyone have any objections?"

No one spoke. Finally Gertrude found words, "I have been given a heavy burden. Such responsibility can only be borne by great leaders such as Silas Barton. Quite honestly, I cannot fully comprehend the full impact of his request on my life or self. There is no way, however, I will be able to handle this alone. Without a total and absolute commitment from every member, I will be forced to decline the position."

Nathan spoke for the group, "The leadership and destiny of PAT is in your hands. You will have the full backing and loyalty from each and every member. Everyone at this table guarantees it."

It was decided that Austin and Tim would play a greater role in the daily running of the store, permitting Gertrude more time for her new position. With renewed zest and a united front, they ended their meeting.

Later in the day, Gert met with Samuel, Rebecca, and Stephen. Though she did not mention PAT specifically, she detailed her latest business plans. "Are you feeling well, Gert?" ventured Rebecca.

"Yes, Rebecca. I'm just fine."

"Then why are you going to be away from the building two days a week?"

"I just need more personal time."

"Are you hiding something from us? This is not at all like you," Sam showed concern in his voice.

"Sam, I told you not to worry," replied Gert.

Stephen did not comment throughout the entire meeting.

Later that evening, when Gert shared her new plan, Dorothy was thrilled to hear she was finally going to take some time off from the store. "This way, you'll take care of yourself." Warmly caressing her hand, she added, "And you'll stay good and healthy—because I want you around for a long, long time."

Gertrude stood outside her apartment building and waited until the car pulled up. "Good morning, Bryan."

"Good morning. We'd better get going; I've got a funny feeling it's going to be a long trip."

"What makes you say that?"

"For some reason, there's been a lot more troop activity this week."

"Any reason for it that we know of?"

"I haven't heard anything on the radio, but it's definitely increased. Nathan was stopped three times—yesterday alone."

"Do you think they suspect anything?"

"No. They appear to be stopping and questioning everyone. We're not being singled out."

As they reached the edge of the city, they encountered a roadblock. As they rolled to a stop, troopers approached their car. Bryan and Gert had agreed she should do the talking.

"Good morning, officer. What seems to be the trouble?" asked Gert in her most innocent voice.

"Just a routine inspection, Madam." Turning his attention to Bryan, he instructed, "Give me the keys to your trunk, please."

While the officer checked the trunk, Gert questioned the other man. "Are you looking for anything in particular?" The officer ignored the question.

"What is your destination?" he said instead.

"My son and I are just taking a short ride to the country to visit my sister."

"That's correct, officer. She's not feeling very well...has some sort of virus," chimed in Bryan inadvertently.

The second officer returned and handed the keys back to Bryan. "Drive slowly and obey the laws."

"Yes, officer, and thank you."

"And, Madam?"

"Yes?"

"I hope your sister feels better," the officer stated as he jotted down their license number on a small pad. They pulled past a long line of waiting cars and stared as the troops walked from vehicle to vehicle.

Gert inquired, "I wonder what's the real cause?"

"Perhaps someone's smuggling contraband into the city?"

"Maybe."

Gertrude's schedule was extremely busy on the days she traveled to PAT's headquarters. Upon arrival, she was escorted and briefed by her principal personnel. Today was no different; she was scheduled to meet with Nathan Morrison and his staff.

Once seated in the small office, they started, "Gert, what are we going to do? Roadblocks are being set up everywhere. Every car and truck is being inspected. I've never seen anything like it; we can't get the manuscripts back to their authors."

"Just hold onto them until things cool down."

"But we're not getting any new books either. The flow is being affected in both directions."

"If that's the case; correspond to all our outside authors and suggest they hold off sending us any more books. I won't be surprised if packages are inspected next. Suggest, also, that they try to work among themselves."

"What do we do then?"

"I'm sure each of you is talented enough to write more books yourselves. We'll have to rely on our in-house staff until the crisis abates."

After meeting with her writing staff, she then spoke with her production editors. Bryan was the first to speak. "We have reduced our production and decreased the run for each book."

"Why?"

"I'm gravely concerned over Andrews' latest activities. Suppose our raw materials get cut off by his roadblocks?"

"Anything is possible. Until that actually occurs, try doubling up on your supply orders."

"I've already tried, but all of our suppliers are also being hampered."

"Try different ones. I know several in the city; I'll call them tomorrow. We can have them deliver the merchandise to my building. We can transport it in small lots; it's not against the law as yet." Then Gert added, "What about other materials?"

"We are running low."

"Try to increase your inventory, and I agree with your decision to reduce production." By the afternoon, she sat at her last meeting. "Any ideas what we should be doing next?" she asked the young faces before her. "We'll continue on Silas' program until we find a change is necessary," she informed them.

Bryan and Gertrude arrived back in time, despite being stopped twice. Gert entered her apartment.

"Have you heard?" Dorothy cried as soon as she saw Gert.

"Heard what?"

"The news about Rebecca?"

"No. What happened?"

"Please sit and I'll tell you." Dorothy took a gulp of wine and then continued. "Rebecca was parking her car this morning. As she stood by the street, she was struck by a car. It was a hit and run."

"Was she hurt?" Gert gasped.

"Thank goodness others were there; they came to her assistance immediately."

"So what happened?"

"Stephen Glasser came down and evaluated the situation. He felt she should be taken to the hospital, but she refused."

"Why didn't she listen?"

"She wanted nothing to do with the government, including their hospitals."

"So what did they do?"

Dorothy took another drink. "Stephen drove her to a friend's office. Austin and I went along to help. Anyhow, when we got there, we learned Stephen is a doctor."

"Yes, I knew that..." Gert said, slightly embarrassed.

"Why didn't you tell me?" Dorothy asked.

"That's not important. Tell me what happened next."

"His friend was away at a conference, so Stephen x-rayed her leg and found her ankle had been fractured. He gave it a fancy Latin name and then proceeded to cast her lower leg. She's walking on crutches."

"How is she doing? A lot of pain?"

"It's under control; Stephen took some medication from his

friend's office and gave it to her."

"Where is she now?"

"Probably at home, but don't call her. She's probably sleeping."

"I'll call her in the morning."

"Forget it. She's already made plans to be back at work tomorrow. You can see her then."

"What about the car that hit her? Did the police find it?"

Taking a deep breath, Dorothy continued. "That's the worse part: She was hit by a police car."

"A police car! How can that be? Are you sure?"

"Positive. Several of our employees saw the whole incident. The car was parked and as soon as Rebecca was within its range, it pulled out, jumped the curb, and hit her."

"Maybe it was an accident..."

"There were no other cars on the street at the time and it was in broad daylight. It was deliberate."

"Why Rebecca?"

"I have no idea."

"Is this the type of thing the Ministry might do?"

"No. They're ruthless, but they're not killers. This was done with the intent to murder her."

"Who else might have done it?"

"I'm not sure, but all of us had better be cautious from now on. They might decide to try it on someone else the next time."

"What should we do?"

"Everyone working in the building is fully aware of what happened. Every employee has been urged to watch out for anything that might appear suspicious. We'll be ready for their next move."

"What does all of this mean?" said Gertrude.

"I just don't know, but I'll tell you one thing: It's a very serious matter."

Holding her younger friend's hand, Gert said, "You really mean that, don't you?"

"I've never been more serious in my life. Somehow—and I

worked for the Ministry for a long time—I believe there is a complex plot against all of us."

"I hope you are wrong, because if you're not, we're all in for a tough time."

FORTY-NINE

Over the next few weeks, subtle changes occurred. Motorists were issued official passes at each roadblock, as inspection stations were strategically constructed throughout the region. The radio merely stated, "It is a temporary measure ordered by Royal Head Commander Andrews." The commentator continued, "Several attempts of civil unrest and the importation of illegal substances have been the Government's primary reasons for implementing such actions. To protect his fine and loyal citizens, such a move by your commander was necessary. In addition to this protective measure, your Government will shortly be issuing travel passes. Further details will be..." he droned on.

To the membership of PAT, these changes meant additional barriers to be negotiated. As quickly as the Government's new passes were distributed, Bryan and his staff printed forgeries. With their counterfeit curfew passes, continuous movement between their two locations was ensured.

A knock at her office door startled Gertrude. "Come in."

"Our mailman Mr. Siffert is here, Miss Johnson," Mary announced from the doorway.

"Please tell him to come right in, Mary." As soon as he entered her office, Gert was at his side. "Thank you for coming, Mr. Siffert."

"My pleasure, Miss Johnson. I haven't seen you in quite some time. I believe it's been a few months. Been busy?"

"Extremely. I have a question to ask you."

"I think I know what you're going to ask, but go ahead and let me see if I'm right."

"Is there something wrong with the mail? The number of orders we've received lately has dropped significantly."

"That is the question I expected. Everyone is having the same problem."

"What's the cause?"

"Officially, we were told to say that any delays would only be temporary and to apologize for any inconvenience. We were also told to announce that the opening of the Postal Service's fifteen new distribution centers has been slightly delayed because of inclement weather and costly overruns."

"I see...that's the official message."

"Yes, Miss Johnson. That's what we've been told to say by our supervisors."

"Mr. Siffert, we've been friends a long time...what's really going on?"

Closing the door behind him, he whispered, "Miss Johnson, I've never seen anything like it. The whole postal system is a mess. The Government has replaced every supervisor and upper management person with military personnel. No one knows what's going on."

"Why?"

"New orders from the very top."

"Royal Head Commander Andrews?"

"That's the rumor going around." Looking nervous, he added, "And there's more."

"What is it?"

"Supposedly, every package and letter is going to be individually inspected."

"But how? That's illegal."

"Not any longer. Royal Head Commander has just passed a new law permitting it."

"What about protocol? How did it pass through the Senate?"

"It didn't. Evidently, he just issued the order and is having his storm troopers enforce it in the name of national security."

"What are we coming to!"

"I know what you mean. Thank goodness, I'll be retiring soon."

"Retiring? Why are you going to retire?"

"Miss Johnson, I'm 55 years old."

"That's not old. We're both in our prime."

"I agree, but the government doesn't."

"Don't tell me! Another of Andrews' new laws?"

"You got it. All mail personnel must retire at the age of 55. This way, they'll be able to replace us with their own people."

"That's quite a plan. Within a few years, they'll control it all."

"It seems that way." He looked concerned. "Miss Johnson, what ever happened to the good old days?"

"Mr. Siffert, I just don't know, but I don't think Andrews is going to make our future any easier."

"I agree...please don't tell anyone what I said."

Later that evening, Dorothy and Gertrude rested in the comfort of their living room. "Gert, you're not going to believe what's happening."

"What now?"

"I went grocery shopping after work today and the store had a sign posted in the front window concerning food stamps."

"What do you mean, food stamps?"

"The government will be issuing food stamps for all its citizens. I overheard several customers saying the few farmers left have had several bad years and there's now a terrible shortage."

"How can that be? Andrews has a five-year plan. And during his last public speech, he indicated the program was well ahead of schedule. They expected a better-than-average crop this year."

"Well, they must have reversed their projections."

"I can't believe this is all happening at once."

"There's more, Gert. Gas rationing will be starting in one month."

"Who told you that?"

"I heard it from Gus at the gas station."

"Is he sure? You know how he gets things mixed up sometimes; especially when it comes to our bill."

"He's already seen samples of the coupons and application forms."

"I think I've heard enough for one day. I wonder what surprises Andrews will have in store for us tomorrow."

It didn't take Gertrude long to find out the leader's newest modifications. After handing her deposits to the teller at her bank, she went into Jasper Farwel's office. As president of the city's largest commercial bank, he could supply information on the recent policy changes.

"Good morning, Gert, have a seat."

"You look troubled, Jasper, what's wrong?"

"I don't understand what's happening, Gert, that's what wrong. We've received at least ten new laws a day during the past week. Every day, the government is changing something else."

"I didn't realize every business was being affected."

"It seems that way. Every statute we've received so far will have enormous impact upon our customers and the way they run their businesses."

"Such as?"

"Within two years, we can expect to be a totally checkless society. The Governmental Banking and Finance Bureau is already manufacturing monetary cards. Citizens will use them instead of cash or checks."

"How can they do it?"

"Simple. After a predetermined date, cash and checks will have no value."

"I can't believe any of this. So much is happening in such a short period of time."

"There's more. Any deposit of over $5,000.00 must be flagged by the bank and a special form must be sent to a central government clearing center."

"Any reason given for the move?"

"Andrews does not have to provide any reason to anybody. He simply makes the rules and we must obey." Gertrude left the bank still confused by recent events. During a meeting with her supervisors, she outlined many of the new changes.

"What are we going to do?" inquired Austin.

"I'm not sure. We'll just have to take one day at a time. There's no other way to do it; you cannot have an organized formula or policy if the rules change on a daily basis. Every time something is altered, we'll study it and modify our program accordingly."

F I F T Y

Dorothy and Austin dined at a restaurant in the heart of the city. After eating, they strolled into a park and sat on one of its concrete benches. While the city's lights and stars blinked overhead, both relaxed. Neither spoke for the longest time; they chose to absorb the scenery.

Finally Austin spoke, "Dorothy, I think we'd better be getting you home."

"Can't we stay a little longer; it's so beautiful?"

"Curfew is in one hour."

"I'm sick and tired of curfews. Don't you have a pass?"

"Not with me. I have some at home."

"Let's go get them. Gert is away and I'm in no rush. Unless you are?"

"Not really; my work is all caught up." They pulled into a parking space in front of his building. "You can wait here if you want; the place is really not fixed up."

"I'd rather come up with you. I'm frightened to stay here alone."

They climbed the five flights. Opening the door, he smiled, "Here it is. My Shangri-La in the heavens."

"I don't know what you were so paranoid about, I think it's cute," Dorothy chuckled.

"Please have a seat and I'll be right out." Instead of sitting, she surveyed his vast compact disc collection. She called to him, "Do you have any recordings by Carol Sogul?"

"Yes. I have the first one she ever did." Returning to the room, he inquired, "Do you like her music?"

"Yes. I saw her in concert years ago."

"What is your favorite song of hers?"

"I love them all, but I'm particularly fond of "Please Don't Ever Forget Me.""

"I used to listen to it all the time. It's one of her better pieces."

"Austin, could I please hear it now?"

"Have a seat and let me see if I can find it." She sat on the sofa while he turned on his audio equipment. After adjusting the volume, he sat at her side and listened to several selections. "I'm sorry. It's been such a long time since I've had company, I almost forgot what to do. Would you like something to drink?"

"Yes, please."

Glancing at his wrist watch, he commented, "Damn, we missed curfew and I can't find any passes. I must have left them in the office."

"It's okay. Why don't we just listen to your records for awhile and then I'll try to make it home myself."

"I'll take you; it'll be safer that way." The atmosphere, soft music, and alcohol soon did their magic.

"Austin, do you have a steady girlfriend?"

"No."

"I'm surprised."

"I'm too involved in my work."

"I understand exactly how you feel; I'm just the same. I can't believe, however, you hardly date. You've got everything a woman could want in a man."

Despite all his attempts to restrain his innermost feelings, Austin broke down and cried. "I'm so sorry; please forgive me. I'm so sorry," he managed to say between sniffs.

Dorothy pulled him to her and gently stroked his hair, "Everything will be just fine. Don't be afraid, just cry and let it all out."

Raising his head, he tearfully looked into her eyes. "Oh, Dorothy, I'm so sad and lonely. Please forgive me." She drew him closer and their lips tenderly touched. He carefully lifted her onto the soft carpeting. They again embraced one another.

"Everything will be just fine," she whispered. "It will be just fine." Again they kissed. As two leaves caught in a whirlpool, they clung to each other.

Throughout the night, they caressed, made love, and held one another affectionately. Finally, at dawn they fell asleep in each other's arms. Dorothy woke before Austin and stared at his handsome features. Smiling, she kissed him lightly on the cheek and quietly walked to the kitchen. Minutes later, Austin awakened to the aroma of freshly cooked bacon and eggs. Walking behind her, he pulled his naked body against hers. Rubbing passionately, he kissed the nape of her neck and whispered, "You smell as good as the food."

Giggling, she responded, "You're impossible, Dr. Mathews." He didn't permit her to escape.

"Come on, Austin, we've got to eat and get to work."

"Let's call in sick and spend the day making wild, passionate love together."

"I can't. There's too much to do."

"How about going in one hour late?"

Smiling, she laughed, "I think that can be arranged." After making love once again, they drove to the store. No one said a word as they leisurely joined the rest of the staff for their morning meeting. Gertrude, who had returned from PAT's headquarters, smiled knowingly as they sat at her side.

"Sorry, we're so late, Gert. Austin and I had a few things to catch up on," Dorothy explained.

Instead of responding, Gert took Dorothy's hand under the table and softly whispered. "I'm glad. It's about time."

FIFTY-ONE

No matter how hard they planned, snags always seemed to develop. A huge shipment of books was being held up in a midwest warehouse. Gertrude was irate. "Why can't we get them here?"

"I've tried everyone," responded Austin.

"Mullins?"

"They're all tied up," he replied.

"I'll never accept it. There has to be a way to get those books here. I've already got them sold."

"What about getting them ourselves? We've done it before; why can't we do it again?" Austin suggested.

"Are there any new laws that would prevent it?" Gertrude inquired of Dorothy.

"I'm not sure. Just hold on for a minute." She called both the Ministry and Department of Transportation. After hanging up, Dorothy said, "Both said it was fine with them as long as our paperwork was filled out properly."

"Good. Where do we get a truck?"

"I have a friend who will loan me his. I'll drive out there and get them."

"I don't want you driving out there alone."

"Let Dorothy come with me," Austin suggested with a grin.

Blushing, she answered, "Austin, please be serious; I'm needed here for inspections."

"Only kidding, Gert. What about Tim?"

"Can we get along with the two of you gone at the same time?" asked Gert.

"It shouldn't be any problem. It'll only take a couple of days." They finalized the arrangements and agreed to leave the following Wednesday.

The night before their departure, Tim and Donna relaxed in their apartment. "Tim, there's something I have to speak to you about," Donna said softly.

"Right now?"

"Yes, my dear. It's rather important." She sat on his lap.

"So what's so important, my little buttercup?"

"Please be serious for once."

"I'm all ears."

"Tim."

"Yes, Donna. What is it already?"

"I'm pregnant."

Suddenly trembling, he asked, "Are you sure?"

"Yes. I saw the doctor yesterday and he confirmed what I already knew."

"When? I mean when is he or she coming?" Tim jumped up from the chair, nearly dropping Donna to the floor.

"Our baby will be arriving next September," she said, after recovering.

He reached down to hold her face. "That's great news!"

"You mean you're not mad or upset?"

Shocked, he answered, "No. Why should I be?"

"I just wasn't sure how you'd react."

Tim eased himself into a kneeling position in front of the chair she now sat in. "I guess this means we'll have to stay together for awhile longer."

"Please be serious. This is important."

"I am, Donna...I think we should make it legal."

"Do you mean it, Tim?"

"Yes...I think we should get married."

Laughing with joy, she responded, "Married!"

"Yes. That legalized institution that sanctions two individuals into a common entity. I think we should do it as soon as I return from this trip." They kissed. "Speaking of trips. Do you want me to cancel my trip with Austin?"

"Why?"

"In case you need me."

"For what? I'm not sick, you know. I'm only having a baby."

"I still don't want you being alone."

"Stop being so old-fashioned and over-protective. I'll be just fine."

"I don't want you here by yourself."

"Okay. I'll call Rhoda and see if I can stay at her place while you're gone."

"Promise?"

"Yes, dear. Anything to keep my husband happy."

Austin picked up Tim before stopping by the store for last minute instructions.

"I want both of you to be extra careful and watch out for any troopers," Gert warned.

"We will, Gert," Austin answered. "Please stop worrying. We'll be back before you even know we're gone."

"It's my nature to be concerned; call it an old woman's pleasure." Hugging each, she added, "And I'll miss both of you very much."

Turning to Dorothy, Austin winked, "See you soon, kid."

She grinned. "Please hurry back safely. Gert and I will miss you." Gathering the completed paperwork, they departed.

To keep herself occupied, Donna decided to work overtime at the store. Mark stuck his head into her doorway. "Hi, Donna, I didn't know you were still here."

"Trying to catch up on some of my work while Tim's away."

"No problem. I'll clean your office later."

"Is Frank around?"

No, Donna. You're the only one left except for me. Everyone went home early today because of the curfew."

"Damn. I totally forgot about it. It's an early night, isn't it?"

"Yes. In fact, it started an hour ago."

"Just great and I don't have a pass."

"I saw some on Austin's desk. Do you want me to get you one?"

"If you don't mind. I'll call my friend and tell her I'll be leaving soon."

Ten minutes later, Mark returned and handed her the pass. "Drive carefully, Donna."

"I will, Mark, and have a good night."

Donna pulled her car onto the empty street and headed along the avenue. A slight breeze stirred as the humid air continued to bake the city. As she turned onto First Street, a red blinking light ahead alerted her to a potential danger. Slowing her car to a crawl, she prayed the troopers would signal her ahead. Since the two officers had nothing to do, they directed her to stop.

Rolling down the window, she looked at the uniformed trooper. "It is past curfew, Madam; please show me your pass." She reached into her pocketbook and handed him the paper. He shown his flashlight directly into her face then proceeded to examine the document. "Please stay here; I'll be right back."

Donna watched nervously as he joined his colleague who was sitting in the patrol car. After a brief conversation, he returned. "Can I please see your license and registration?"

"Is there anything wrong, officer?"

He repeated his question in a monotone voice. "Can I please

see your license and registration?"

"I'm in an awful rush, officer. I've got to get home to my family."

Shining the light into her face, he stated, "I want to see them right now." She removed the papers from her wallet and handed them to him. He walked back to his co-officer and again conversed for several minutes.

Donna was becoming extremely uncomfortable. With no other cars in sight, the desolate street seemed like her worse nightmare. She was remembering Rebecca's fate. Scanning the area for any sign of life, she silently prayed, *Please, somebody come along.*

"Miss, could you please step out of your car."

She looked at the officer. "Get out of the car? Why? Is anything wrong?"

"Please get out of your car."

She opened the door and stood. "What's wrong, officer?"

"This pass is a fake. It's not real."

"There must be some mistake, officer." Placing the document on the hood of her car, he shown the light onto the pass.

After pointing out several printing errors, he continued. "In fact, this is one of the worst forgeries my partner and I have ever seen."

"Please. I didn't have any idea. Honestly, I must have gotten it by mistake."

"Where did you get it?"

"I can't remember." Shaking slightly, she answered, "I'm just nervous right now."

"I can understand how you must feel, but you have just broken two governmental laws. One is trying to give us a fake pass and the second is being out after curfew without a pass."

"Let me go, my family—"

"I'm very sorry, Miss, but as officers entrusted to uphold the laws of our fine country, I'm afraid we can't honor that request."

"What are you going to do with me?"

"We're going to take you to headquarters for further questioning."

Openly crying, she pleaded, "Please, officer, don't do this to me. I promise—"

"You should have thought about it before you decided to break the law." The other trooper exited the patrol car and walked to his side. "Trooper Germansky will drive you in his car; I'll follow behind in yours."

"I can't believe this is happening. Please let me go."

"Just come along peacefully; we don't want any trouble from you." They locked her in the rear section of their patrol car. The driver slowly drove Donna's car behind the official government sedan. They drove for fifteen minutes before their passenger questioned, "Where are you taking me?"

"To headquarters."

"But you're heading out of town."

The officer did not respond.

"Did you hear what I said? We're going in the wrong direction."

"We're taking you to an auxiliary station, just relax."

"Can't you just let me go?"

"Sorry, Miss. I just follow orders."

They pulled off the highway into a deserted, wooded tract of land.

"What is this?" shouted Donna. "This isn't the police station." They stood outside the cars and spoke. During this time, Donna frantically attempted to unlock the door. "Please! Please let me go!"

After deciding their next move, they dragged her physically from the vehicle and forced her onto the cool ground. "Please!" she screamed. "Let me go!"

"Tell us where you got that forgery," one officer demanded.

"I don't know!" she screamed uncontrollably, "I don't know!" Finding she couldn't break their grasp, she attempted to wiggle herself free from her captors.

"Hold her tightly while I get her clothes off. I'll show her who's boss. By the time we're done with her, she'll tell us everything we want to know." Within seconds, they stripped her entire body. As she screamed, they held her tighter and proceeded to rape and sodomize their helpless young victim. During the course of the multiple repulsive acts of violence, Donna deliberately bit one of her attackers on his hand. The trooper winced in pain and reflexively picked up a nearby rock. Furious, he smashed it onto her head. Within a moment, her body lay flaccid and bleeding. After reaching the culmination of their pleasure, the two troopers dressed and plotted their next move.

Gertrude picked up her phone and turned instantly ashen.

"What's wrong, Gert?" inquired Dorothy from across the room.

With a weakened voice, she answered, "Dorothy, it's Donna; she's dead."

"Dead! How? We just saw her tonight in the store."

"They found her dead in her car. She had been raped and then murdered."

"Do they know who did it?"

"It's under investigation by the government, but so far, they have no leads."

"Poor Tim."

"I'll make all the arrangements. Austin and Tim are due back tomorrow; I'll break the news to Tim," Gert said sadly.

The two men arrived precisely on schedule. Gertrude quickly summoned them into her office. There she told them the tragic news. The very next day Donna was buried alongside Silas Barton. Tim, throughout this period, did not speak or shed a single tear. Instead, he stood motionless and passive as his longtime confidant and lover was laid to rest.

Three days later Gertrude pulled Austin aside. "Has anyone seen Tim?"

"No, Gert. I've called his apartment, but no one answered."

"Austin, I'm very concerned."

"So is all the staff. In fact, a couple of us were going to stop by after work and see how he is doing. I'll try to gently nudge him back to work; it'll be good for him to keep busy."

"Call me at home and let me know how he's doing."

Around 8:00 that evening, the phone rang and Dorothy picked it up. She spoke for several minutes in a shallow voice. Finally, she put down the phone and started to weep.

"What is it?" Gertrude asked.

Sobbing, she cried, "Tim's dead!"

"Did you say 'Tim's dead'?"

"Yes. That was Austin. When they got to his apartment, he didn't answer the bell. They got a spare key from the landlord and let themselves in. They found him dead in the tub."

"I don't believe it," Gert said quietly. "I just don't believe any of it."

"He slashed his wrists with a razor and died."

"Oh, Gert, when is this going to end? I don't know how much more of this I can take." They held one another, each trying to comfort the other.

FIFTY-TWO

Gertrude delivered a short eulogy and watched as Tim's casket was lowered into the ground next to the fresh grave of his partner. She and Dorothy then attempted to console Austin who was taking his friend's death extremely hard. Instead of returning to her apartment, Dorothy decided to stay with Austin. Fearing for Austin's very life, she and Gert monitored his every move. For days, he required their complete attention and friendship and it took more than three full weeks before the business began to demonstrate any sign of returning to normal.

The phone rang and Gert picked it up after the first ring. "Stephen, what can I do for you?"

"Just turn on your radio," he urged. "Hurry up."

After hanging up, she reached back, turned the switch, and listened. "Today is a sad moment in our country's history: Our Royal Head Commander Andrews died at 3:45 a.m. He expired peacefully in his sleep. Assuming temporary control as Head of State will be General Virgil Daniels. Further details and announcements will be broadcast throughout the day." A moment of silence filled the airways followed by the country's national anthem. Gertrude walked quickly to Austin's office. "Did you hear the news?"

"No."

"Andrews is dead."

Leaning forward in his chair, Austin spoke, "He's dead? Thank God."

"Let's not prejudge the situation; the news may not be that good."

"I'm afraid you're losing me."

"We don't know who will be named as his successor. We only know that a General Daniels will assume temporary control."

"General Daniels," Austin moaned. "He's got a terrible reputation. Supposedly, he's a worse tyrant."

"Have the radio played through the speaker system. I want everyone to hear what is said," Gertrude requested. She walked towards the door, asking "Where will you be?"

"I'm going to speak to Dorothy, but let's have a general meeting in about one hour." He then arranged for the announcements to be heard throughout the building.

The meeting was quickly called to order. "Gertrude, what shall we do now?" inquired Nathan.

"I'm not sure."

Their conversation was interrupted by another broadcast: "General Daniels has officially announced that the funeral arrangements for our Royal Head Commander Andrews have been finalized. Services will begin tomorrow at 8:00 a.m. In honor of our fallen leader, the General has declared tomorrow a National Day of Mourning. All businesses and services are to be closed and no traveling except for emergencies will be permitted.

Royal Head Commander Andrews' only son, Paul, is on his way from Zarka. He is expected to arrive sometime tonight at the National Airport. Paul studied International Law and was doing post-graduate studies in that country. Upon hearing of his beloved father's death, Paul boarded a plane and is returning to his native soil."

Another announcer spoke, "Being the last living member of our ruling class, it is assumed that Paul will take full control of our country once our great leader's funeral services have been completed." Seconds after the last commentator spoke, music again filled the room.

"Just great!" shouted Austin. "Another Andrews!"

Gert asked, "Does anyone know anything about Paul?"

"Not much," answered Bryan. "He's sort of an enigma. I've heard he is a highly intelligent individual who became rather rebellious during his adolescence. To smooth out his rough edges, he was sent abroad to further his education."

"How old is he?" asked Gert.

Dorothy responded, "I'm not exactly sure, but he's probably in his mid-thirties...of course, that's only a guess."

Austin sarcastically remarked, "He's probably a chip off his old man's block. Remember the old saying: Like father, like son."

Bryan added, "I see no reason to dispute that, every Andrews who has ever ruled this country has been a dictator. Each has governed with a totally iron fist." He added, "The acorns don't fall far from the oaks."

Every mouth silenced and every ear listened as another announcement was generated from the radio: "General Daniels has just announced that the entire Senate has resigned. Their resignations are effective immediately. Senators offered no comments when interviewed. Each confirmed the General's statement. General Daniels has also decreed that all regular curfew hours have been suspended. The new curfew will be between the hours of 7:00 p.m. and 6:00 a.m. These new times will be rigidly enforced by our governmental troops. All passes are no longer valid. In the case of an emergency during this period, call your local police for assistance."

Gertrude studied everyone's reaction to the latest changes. Bryan was the first to speak. "What about the business?"

"It seems everything is going to be operating at a greatly reduced rate," Gert began, "Nobody is singling us out; it's going to affect everyone and every business in this country." She then turned to Dorothy. "Why do you think this is happening?"

"I can't even guess. It's not a logical move as far as government strategy. I never heard anything like it in all my years of studying governmental policies. It's contrary to all the theories I ever learned."

Austin added, "What about our rights as citizens?"

Dorothy quickly interjected, "At this point, citizens no longer have any individual rights. You now have a true tyranny in the making. General Daniels is calling all the shots."

Gertrude commented, "Perhaps we should request that our staff live here for awhile. We have enough room for everyone and we can get enough supplies to easily hold us through this crisis."

Dorothy agreed. "That might be the best solution. That way, we will all be relatively safe from the troopers and can at least form a united front." Everyone approved the motion.

Once the meeting adjourned, Dorothy pulled Gert aside. "That was a terrific idea; we have showers and all the facilities we need."

"I'm just terribly concerned for my staff. Ever since Donna's murder, I've been very uneasy."

Another radio message stopped their conversation: "General Daniels has just decreed that he will be setting up a temporary government to reign over our country's daily affairs. Additionally, our great General has announced the complete and total blackout of any further news. To comply with General Daniels' command, this station will cease all future broadcasting until the mandate has been lifted by the General himself."

A heavy silence filled the room. Dorothy looked disturbed, "I don't like any of this!"

"Neither do I. I'm going to speak to Stephen, Rebecca, and Samuel. Let's see what they think."

"I'll see you later, Gert. I'd better go help the others. The faster we secure the building, the happier I'll be."

After speaking to Gertrude, the other tenants agreed to enact a similar strategy.

Every day, things seemed to get worse for the public. After Royal Head Commander Andrews was laid to rest, General Daniels remained in full control of the populace. Every temporary restriction became permanent and new laws were decreed on a daily basis. With mail delivery down to a fraction of its original volume, most of the bookstore staff spent time checking inventory or lecturing among themselves or to the public.

Travel was nearly impossible as the number of roadblocks increased significantly. Gas supplies were diminished and rationing coupons were instituted. Most people waited in long lines for food or reduced their consumption. With transportation impeded, produce and supplies in and out of the larger cities became scarce and often unobtainable. Every aspect of human life was influenced.

Greater numbers of troopers patrolled the streets of the city. This situation caused the majority of the building's staff to remain indoors. Without radio or other media, the citizens had no idea what was happening elsewhere or within the government itself.

Though no major injuries or illnesses occurred, Stephen was able to handle minor medical problems. Because of the restricted travel, Gert was unable to travel to PAT's headquarters. No matter how hard they tried, no contact could be made with their fellow members in the cave. Gertrude could only hope Bryan and Nathan could hold the operation together without her direction.

With military helicopters and jet planes flying overhead on a regular basis and troopers stationed on every corner, it appeared General Daniels was slowly tightening his grip on the nation. Dorothy bore a great deal of the burden during this time. She was not only expected to deal with the building's overall security, but also tried to outguess the government's next move. Because deliveries and business had declined, inspections were diminished by the Ministry.

One day Major Whittington sat in her office. He looked over

her paperwork and approved her forms. Upon completing the task, he spoke. "Miss Clifton, I'm not sure when I'll be back."

"Major Whittington, what do you mean?"

Inching forward in his chair and looking nervously around the room, he whispered, "Dorothy, I just don't know what's going on."

"In what way?"

"Everything is in turmoil within the department. Nobody wants to make a decision. From the very top to the very bottom, everything is a mess."

Showing concern, she asked, "Walter, what are you going to do?"

"What can I do? I've simply got to ride out the storm. At least three-quarters of Andrews' supporters are gone. All were immediately replaced by the General's personnel. It's a terrible way to live."

"I know how you feel."

"Actually, Dorothy, you were quite lucky."

"Me? Lucky?"

"Yes. You got out just in time. In many ways, I'm envious of you."

"Why don't you just quit?"

"And do what? I have a wife and family to support. Who wants to hire a former government inspector anyhow? I don't think my chances for employment are too great in today's marketplace."

"I guess I'm luckier than I think."

"You're not just lucky, Dorothy; you're the luckiest person I know." Leaning back in his chair, he inquired, "By the way, have you heard anything from your parents?"

"Not a word."

"That's too bad. I did hear through the grapevine they might be in some trouble."

"What kind?" Dorothy asked quickly.

"Evidently General Daniels and your father are not seeing eye to eye on several items. I wouldn't be surprised if he's forced to resign his position shortly."

"I hope you're wrong; it would just kill both of them. My parents have devoted their entire lives to this country. They deserve better."

"Unfortunately with General Daniels in control, patriotism is a thing of the past."

Dropping her head to her chest, Dorothy stated, "It's a whole new world, Walter."

He sighed, "I'd better be going, Dorothy. Hopefully I'll see you again."

"Walter?"

"Yes?"

Catching his eyes, she said, "Best of luck, and do me a favor."

"Anything."

"If you see my parents, tell them I still love them very much."

"I will for sure." Dorothy watched the Major leave. Despite all their philosophical differences, she understood his conflict and pain. His own system was his downfall. She walked directly to Gert's office. Once inside, she warmly hugged her friend.

Surprised by the unexpected affection, Gert quipped, "What's that for?"

"Just a little hug to thank you."

Grinning, Gert jested, "The whole world is falling apart and you thank me now?" They laughed and momentarily relaxed. "How did the inspection go?" asked Gert.

"No problem; we passed as usual."

"That's why I hired you in the first place. Few people could handle the Major as you do. You're just sensational."

"You're so right, but don't forget even majors are human." Gertrude did not know what had prompted Dorothy's last statement, but chose not to question its meaning.

FIFTY-THREE

"When do you think it will stop raining?" Austin asked Gert idly.

"I'm not sure, Austin, but who cares? We're dry in here."

"That's true, but it's been raining for three straight days. Enough is enough."

"Think of the positive side: It keeps the planes out of the air and troops off the streets."

"Come to think of it, you're right. I guess the rain is good after all."

"And remember, there's sometimes a rainbow at the end of a storm."

"Seeing is believing."

The intercom interrupted their conversation. "Yes, Mary, what is it?"

"Dorothy would like Austin to come downstairs when he has a free moment."

Smiling, Gert remarked, "Don't keep her waiting, I'll speak to you later."

Minutes later, Mary knocked and entered. "Miss Johnson, I almost forgot again."

"Forgot what?"

"This." She handed her a sealed envelope. "Ralph found it under the front door this morning."

"Thank you, Mary."

As soon as the door closed, Gertrude opened the correspondence: "Bring a copy of the Bible and *Divine Comedy* to our usual meeting place tonight. Be there at 5:00 sharp."

I can't believe it; I just don't believe it. With anticipation, Gert called one of her clerks. Within one hour, both books were sitting on her desk. She reread the letter once more, then ripped it into several small pieces, and threw it into the trash can. Sitting back, she stared at the books. *Why is he back? Why did he ask this time for specific titles?*

After a rather grueling staff meeting, Austin stayed behind to chat with Gert. "Look, Austin, the rain's letting up," she remarked.

"I'm glad; I thought we'd have to build an ark."

"I'm happy also. I've got to go out for a little while."

He quickly asserted, "Outside! It's not safe. Let me go instead."

"You can't," Gertrude stated with finality.

"Where are you going?" he persisted.

"I have to deliver these books to someone."

"I'll take them for you."

"No. I have to do it myself."

"Gert, between the troopers and the rain, I'll worry while you're gone."

"Everything will be just fine. It's only a short distance away and my friend—"

"Your friend is back?"

"Yes."

"How is she feeling?"

"I'm not exactly sure. I haven't seen her in quite some time."

"Did she say anything about any of the other books?"

"No. Why do you keep asking?"

"No specific reason. It's just that you take such great pain in selecting her books, I was just curious." Austin backpedaled, hoping he hadn't revealed his anxiety.

"Today, she's getting a copy of the Bible and *Dante's Divine Comedy - I. Inferno.*"

"That's quite an interesting combination."

"I agree. I'll bring them to her and come right back."

"Don't visit too long; remember the new curfew."

"You worry too much." Noticing it was nearing 4:30 p.m. Gertrude placed the two books into a plain brown shopping bag and went outside. Several storm troopers, seeking shelter under a nearby awning, glanced at the old woman carrying a small bag, but decided she posed no probable threat to national security. Though the intense rain had abated, a gentle drizzle still fell upon the earth.

Entering the empty park, the clicking of Gert's heels against the wet pavement reverberated. As she reached her destination, Gert noticed she was isolated and fully exposed. Clutching her raincoat tightly and repositioning her umbrella, the elderly woman sat and waited on the wooden bench. 5:05 p.m. and still the stranger had not appeared....

Minutes later, she heard a series of footsteps and observed two men entering the park. They stopped momentarily, then proceeded to walk in her direction. Each stood over six feet in height and appeared well-built. Upon reaching the bench, they stopped. They surveyed the area once again and then stared at the tiny woman. The taller of the two spoke. "What is your name?"

Looking upward, she nervously responded, "My name? Why are you asking?"

"Your name?"

"Are you with the government?" Not observing any uniforms or badges of authority, Gert continued. "I think I'd better be going. I'm late and want to get home before the curfew starts."

Blocking her way, he repeated his question. "What is your name?"

"Gertrude Johnson."

"Show us proof."

"Why? What right do you have to ask?" Though still frightened, she held her ground. "Who are you?"

"I want to see the proof." She handed him her national registration card and watched as he carefully studied its picture and personal description sections. He then handed it back to her. "What's in the bag?"

"A gift—"

"To who?"

"A friend."

"What is it?"

"It's none of your business. It's only a gift." One of the men took the bag and withdrew the two books. After reading their titles, he returned them to her.

He raised his watch to his mouth and whispered, "It's her."

"I really must be going; I'm very late." They easily blocked her escape. As she was about to shout for help, a car entered the park. Slowly, the black stretch limousine drove towards where the three were standing. It stopped and a rear door opened. Another tall, muscular man exited and studied Gert's small frame. He gestured and one of his accomplices took the paper bag away.

"That's mine. Please give it back to me," Gert asserted.

"Get in the car."

"I will not."

"I said get in the car right now."

Realizing any form of escape was physically impossible, she asked, "Who are you? Am I under arrest?"

Reaching into his pocket, he withdrew the handle of a revolver. "I will not ask again, Miss Johnson. Get in the car." After Gertrude settled herself into the back seat, the limo exited the park and maneuvered along the streets of the city.

"Why are you doing this? Where are you taking me?" The three men sat stone-faced. "You can't go around kidnapping peo-

ple against their will. It's illegal." Sensing she was getting nowhere, Gert sat back, clutched the bag to her chest, and looked out the window.

The vehicle raced along the avenues and highways. For the next two hours, no one spoke a word or uttered a sound. The tinted windows hindered her vision and prevented anyone from peering in as the car passed. Studying her three abductors, Gert found each emotionless, expressionless, offering only an austere, mask-like appearance. Finally the vehicle came to a stop. The doors opened, and the three men exited.

"We're here, Miss Johnson, please get out." Realizing she had no choice, Gert stepped out of the car and followed her kidnappers.

"What are we going to do?" Dorothy wailed.

"Please try to relax, Dorothy. I'm sure there's a reasonable explanation for Gert's temporary disappearance," Austin tried to console her.

"Austin, you're not speaking to a child. Don't play games with me; I know you're worried too."

"What can we do? We've checked everywhere. It's as if she's been swallowed up by the earth itself. Not a trace or clue anywhere," Austin was guilt-stricken, remembering the mistaken bags of books. They examined the torn, handwritten letter. "Can you make anything out of it?" Austin asked.

"Nothing. There's not enough information. It's just too damn vague."

Holding Dorothy in his arms, Austin said, "Dorothy, we're trying. We're doing everything within our power to find her."

She sobbed, "Please, Austin. I'm frightened something terrible has happened. Please find her." Austin realized the two most important women in his life were relying on him.

Gertrude awoke sometime during the next day. She recalled being ushered into a farmhouse despite her rather boisterous

protests. Without responding to any of her objections or demands, the three guards escorted her to the basement and locked her in a large room. Since the room was underground, Gert could not judge what time of day or night it was. The room was pleasantly decorated with all the amenities present for a comfortable level of survival. Banging on the heavy metal door with her fist and shouting loudly, Gert failed to elicit any response.

Realizing such actions were non-productive, she sat on the bed and attempted to come up with a reasonable explanation for her predicament. Her thoughts were interrupted by the door suddenly opening. One of her abductors entered, carrying a tray of food. He placed it on the table and relocked the door behind him. "We thought you might be hungry."

"That's awfully nice of you. How do I know it's not poisoned?" came Gert's sharp reply.

Without a hint of emotion, he commented, "It's good. If our goal was to kill you, we could have done it in the park. We did not have to go to all this trouble."

She walked to the table. "What is the purpose of my being here? Am I under arrest?"

"I'm not at liberty to say."

"What kind of answer is that? You kidnap me, lock me up like a caged animal, and then give me a dumb response like that. Tell me, young man, why am I here?"

"I'm not at liberty to say."

"Who are you and who is responsible for this?"

"I'm not at liberty to say."

"Are you a human being or a parrot? Don't you know any other words?" He did not respond to her verbal attack, neither altering his expression, nor losing his temper.

Instead, he calmly replied, "I suggest you eat before it gets cold."

"Perhaps, I will decide not to eat. Maybe I'll go on a hunger strike like Gandhi and die."

"Gandhi did not die from starvation and should you elect to do something that stupid, it'll be solely your decision and not ours. Our purpose is not to kill you."

"Then what is your purpose?"

"I'm not at liberty to say."

"Can you at least tell me where I am?"

"No."

"Great! There's nothing like a logical conversation with yourself. How long will I be kept here?"

"I am not—"

Cutting him off, she mimicked his voice, "I already know your answer. You're not at liberty to say. Correct?" Pausing slightly, she continued sarcastically, "Is there anything we can discuss?"

"No. Not at this time."

"Fine. Let me know when I can talk to someone." She sampled the food and found it quite palatable. "Did you cook this?"

"Yes."

"Have you done a lot of cooking before?"

"Yes."

"At least we're speaking to one another. May I call my store and tell them I'm safe?"

"No."

"But my staff will be worried."

"It is not necessary."

"Why not? They're my friends. Can you at least tell them I'm alive?"

"No."

She remained silent and finished eating the food. Soon after, the guard removed the tray and relocked the door. The next few days were carbon copies. Despite all her attempts, Gert could not extract any information from her captors. To pass time and save her sanity, she read from the two books and wrote down her thoughts.

Her concentration was broken by the entrance of two men. Each carried several boxes. They placed them on her bed and quickly left without a word. Later, they returned with several others.

"We thought you could use these," was their only comment.

Gert opened one of the cartons. "These are my clothes. But how...how did you get them?"

Glaring at each man, she screamed, "You stole them from my apartment, didn't you?"

"Yes."

She proceeded to open the other boxes and discovered that most of her belongings and personal goods were present. Reaching into the last container, her hand abruptly came upon a hard object. Quickly she withdrew a book: *Moby Dick*. "Where did you get this book?" she demanded.

"It's not important."

"Oh, yes it is. This book did not come from my apartment." Neither man showed any response.

"I said this book did not come from my apartment. It was given to a very special person. How did you get it from him?"

"I'm afraid—"

"Don't double talk me! How did you get this book? If you hurt him in any way, I'll get even. Do you understand me?" Again Gert shouted, "If you hurt him at all, I'll kill both of you! Do I make myself perfectly clear?" Without responding or turning back, they exited the room.

FIFTY-FOUR

Austin answered his phone.

"Please come over to our apartment—fast."

"Dorothy, what's wrong? Calm down and tell me."

Instead, she broke down. "Please, Austin, just come over." He rushed to her apartment. Upon opening the door, he stood in near shock. The entire dwelling was bare; nothing was left except the telephones. Walking into the empty living room, Austin found Dorothy sitting on the bare, hardwood floor. Holding her tightly, he attempted to comfort her quaking body.

"I can't take any more," she cried. "First Gert and now this." The phone disturbed the silence and he snatched it up. He spoke for several minutes and then returned to her side. "Was it news about Gert?"

"No. It was Mary."

"What did she want?"

"Some of the staff called in from their homes; all have been ransacked and gutted."

Dorothy sat upright. "Like this?"

"Yes. Let's go to my place and see what's there." A short time later, they found his apartment like all the others—void of any contents.

"Austin, what's this all about?"

"I'm not sure, but let's get back to the store fast." By the time they arrived, all 123 employees had reported being robbed.

At an emergency meeting for everyone in the building, it was determined all had experienced a similar fate. Before the shocked and bewildered crowd, Austin called for order, then spoke, "The past few weeks have been one of the most disturbing times of my entire life. It started with Gertrude's unexpected disappearance, and culminated with today's robberies.

Since our lives are possibly in grave danger, I am going to suggest the following plan: We must be continually on the lookout for potential perils. In fact, our complex of buildings must be protected against all possible threats. It seems to me the store is the only safe haven we still have. Under Dorothy's leadership, security shifts must be organized and implemented immediately. We must have seven-days-a-week, twenty-four-hours-a-day protection. Except for purchasing essentials, no one should leave the buildings. Those with loved ones should have them move in with us. I believe they'll also be safer here.

"I cannot fully comprehend what is occurring; however, we must be better prepared for whatever may happen next. Gertrude would have wanted it this way."

Looking at the group, he asked, "Are there any objections?" Finding no dissension, they hastily terminated the meeting and set about executing the plan. With all the discouragement in their lives, each member attempted to keep their spirits up, but found the chore difficult.

At precisely 4:00 a.m. a large, unmarked truck slowly rolled down the street and parked in front of the bookstore. Keeping its engine running and lights off, it remained stationary. Moments later, another truck pulled behind the first. Shortly, the entire street was filled by a hundred or so unmarked vehicles.

Ralph, during his routine security check, looked out the window of the bookstore. He didn't think twice about the first two trucks parked in front of the store, but as the others followed, he instinctively realized something was very wrong. Running as fast as he could, Ralph picked up the nearest wall phone. In a sleepy tone, Austin responded, "What is it?"

"Look out your window."

Seconds later, Austin inquired, "How long have they been there?"

"It started not long ago. I have a really bad feeling, Austin."

"So do I. Get everyone downstairs." As the vehicle build-up continued, the entire group sat nervously in the basement. Austin arrived and stood on a nearby table. "Stay calm. Remain here and just don't panic." Turning to Dorothy, he questioned, "Are all the alarms set?"

"Yes. Everything is ready." The roaring of truck engines resounded among the tall buildings. Overhead a single helicopter flew. With its noise muted by the loud sounds, it landed on the building's flat roof. After rapidly unloading troops and supplies, the chopper returned to the night skies. Seven others followed suit.

While their victims sat quietly in the basement, the special assault team finalized plans for their attack. At a prearranged time and with flawless precision, they began their assault. Air vents were pried open and a sleeping gas infiltrated the building's ventilation system. With all the windows tightly sealed, the silent offensive intensified quickly. Within a few short minutes, every living thing in the complex was unconscious.

A single beam of light overhead signaled the beginning of the next maneuver. Electrical systems were disconnected until the debugging and security specialists surveyed and cleared the entire building. Free of any danger, hundreds of troops poured out of the parked trucks and systematically ran into the complex. The striking of their heels echoed along the street as each soldier raced to an assigned position. Each and every door was forcibly opened and removed. Free of obstacles, the rampage of the structure began.

Each sleeping victim was securely tied and gagged. Without any difficulty, every individual was then placed on a stretcher and carried into one of the waiting trucks. As the last captive was lifted onto a vehicle and secured, the truck pulled away into the darkness.

For the next several days, the troopers worked around the clock to remove everything from the buildings. Every last item was carefully stored, labeled, and loaded into a truck. At the end, the commander-in-chief and his staff rechecked the empty rooms. Satisfied, everyone left. With its doors and windows broken, the complex became an eyesore to the recently rehabilitated neighborhood and within a few short hours, government troopers reclaimed the building as a new police station and headquarters.

Precisely as that first truck stopped in front of Gertrude's Bookstore, a large military helicopter secretly landed in a small clearing. Several others followed. The elite division headed towards the cave's entrance. Donning masks, they proceeded to inject a sleeping gas into the large portal of the ventilation system. Within minutes, everyone in PAT's subterranean headquarters was unconscious. Each member was bound, gagged, and carried back to the clearing.

The helicopters soon returned and transported the soldiers and their hostages to a predetermined location. During the next few days, the area was filled with activity: With all the land mines and hidden explosives neutralized on either side of the path, a bulldozer widened the dirt area leading to the cave. Books, presses, furnishings, and other machinery were painstakingly packed and loaded onto the waiting trucks. As the last vehicle pulled away, all evidence of PAT's existence had been eliminated. It was as if nothing had been in the cave for years. Nothing now stirred except the brook below and birds overhead.

F I F T Y - F I V E

The door swung open causing Gert to awaken abruptly from a long overdue, tranquil sleep. She watched as her guard carried in a small, portable cot. "What's that for?" Gert demanded.

As usual, he did not respond to her question. She sat up and asked again. "I said, what's that for?" Before another word could cross her lips, two guards carried a young woman into the room and placed her unconscious body on the cot. Gertrude was on her feet and shoving the men aside. "What have you done to her? So help me, I'll kill you...." The two exited and relocked the door before she could even finish her threat. Gert removed Dorothy's gag and untied the ropes that confined her extremities. Noticing her friend was breathing regularly and not in any apparent distress, she attempted to wake her from the extremely deep repose. Despite all attempts, nothing worked. *If they did anything to hurt you, so help me, I'll kill them myself.* For hours Gert held her sleeping friend's hand hoping to shelter her. Sometime later, Dorothy stirred. Gert gently nudged her on the arm. "Wake up."

Moving slightly, she opened her eyes. "Gert?"

"Yes, it's me." They held each other tightly and cried for joy.

"I thought you were dead. I was so worried." After a lengthy, tearful reunion, the two sat and reviewed the previous events.

"The store?"

"I haven't any idea, Gert. All I remember is falling asleep."

"And Austin?"

"I haven't any idea about anyone." Dorothy stood and walked around the room. "Where are we?"

"Your guess is as good as mine."

"And those men?"

"No idea."

Dorothy checked for any surveillance devices, but found none. "It makes no sense at all; why didn't they just kill us? Why go to all this trouble?" Gert couldn't provide her with an adequate answer. "We've got to figure out a way to escape."

"I'm not sure it's possible," Gert commented. "There's an awful lot of them and only two of us."

"We've got to at least try." For the next few hours they schemed. Finally, they came up with a plan.

"Once we're out of the room, we still don't know what we're going to face," Gert pointed out.

"I know, Gert, but we can't spend the rest of our lives in this room." Hearing movement in the hallway, Dorothy quickly grabbed a heavy, wooden chair and stood in a strategic location behind the door. Gertrude nervously sat on her bed and watched as the door inched inward.

"Food! Please bring it in; I'm starving," Gert coaxed nonchalantly. The guard was about to enter, but stopped abruptly. Instinctively, he scanned the room.

Without the least hint of fear, he spoke: "Tell your friend to put down the chair and to come out from behind the door. I will not come any farther until she is sitting at your side." Realizing their plan had failed, Dorothy did as directed.

The guard placed the food on their table. "Escape is impossible. Forget any foolish notions you might have. You are too well guarded."

Dorothy retorted, "You expect us to sit here and listen to you?"

"I gave you sound advice. It is a total waste of your time and energy to try to escape. The whole area is heavily secured by armed guards."

Trying to obtain more information, Dorothy asked, "You're a storm trooper, aren't you?"

"I am not at liberty to say."

"I used to work for the government; I believe I saw your I.D. in our master file. Am I correct?"

With no sentiment, he answered, "I'm not at liberty to say."

"What are you at liberty to tell me?"

Closing the door behind him, he responded to the younger woman's question, "Nothing."

When he returned to pick up the empty lunch tray, the guard spoke again, "Turn on your radio in a few minutes."

"Why?" asked Gert.

"I'm not at liberty to say."

"Perhaps they're going to have a song dedicated in our honor?" jested Dorothy.

"I suggest you turn it on," the guard repeated flatly.

After he had left, Gert switched on the radio. Static filled the room as they waited. A male voice suddenly broke the silence. "Good afternoon, listeners. This is James Tobin and I'll be the host of today's show. Before we begin our musical selections, Captain Michael Taylor, the official head of our government's public relations department has several important announcements."

After a slight pause, he continued, "Effective yesterday at 12:00 p.m., General Daniels and his entire military staff have resigned as head of our government. Effective immediately, General Daniels has retired because of personal and health reasons.

"Assuming his rightful position as head of our government will be Royal Head Commander Paul Andrews, only son of our late great leader Andrews. Within the next few days, Royal Head Commander Paul will deliver his first live, state-of-the-nation address.

"On behalf of our new administration, we wish to offer the very best to General Daniels and his staff. It is hoped that his health improves and we thank him for his support and assistance during this transitional period." Music followed.

"What do you think?" asked Gert.

"Without any facts, I cannot even venture a guess."

"What will this mean to us?"

"I'm not sure. Perhaps Royal Head Commander Paul will respect his father's previous edicts and we'll be permitted to operate the store under your grandfather clause. Who knows?"

"Do you think Paul will be worse than General Daniels?"

"I can't imagine anything being as bad, but remember we're dealing with a completely unknown factor."

"I never felt so damn helpless in all my life. I feel as if my entire destiny is in someone else's hands." They spoke and listened continuously for any further news, but nothing specific was announced. It seemed the nation was just waiting for Royal Head Commander Paul's initial speech. Days passed and both Dorothy and Gertrude attempted to keep themselves occupied. Each read the two books and then exchanged ideas about the authors' techniques.

"It's really too bad you didn't have an opportunity to study literature in school. You're quite a natural," Gert observed.

"It's too bad I couldn't see what I see now," Dorothy agreed.

"Perhaps things sometimes turn out for the best anyway."

Looking at her surroundings, Dorothy laughed, "I hope that excludes this place."

Sometime later, the guard delivered them another meal. Dorothy started asking him a multitude of questions. "Do you have any idea when Royal Head Commander Paul is speaking?" Glancing at his watch, he answered, "Fifty-five minutes."

"Have you ever met him?"

227

"I'm not at liberty to say."

"Do you have a name? After all this time, I hate to be so formal."

"It is of no concern at this point. Perhaps at some other time."

Gertrude spoke up. "Other time? What do you mean by that?"

"I'm not at liberty to say," he stated as he left the room.

Both women sat by the small table and listened intently to the radio. "I never thought I'd be waiting to hear someone speaking on the radio," Gert admitted.

Dorothy smiled. "I know what you mean."

The music finally stopped and an announcer spoke. "Fellow citizens. We are now broadcasting live and uncensored from Liberty Hall. From my position, I can see our new leader, Royal Head Commander Paul making his way up to the podium." The background echoed with applause and shouting. "In a few moments, you will hear our newest Royal Head Commander deliver his first public speech." After pausing, the commentator continued, "it appears he's almost ready...." Suddenly, static flooded the airways. The two women looked aghast at one another. Dorothy grabbed the small radio, but despite all her attempts, no coherent sound was emitted, only static.

Gert moaned, "I can't believe it." They continued to stare at the radio in disgust. Fifteen minutes later, music again filled their ears.

Later in the day, Dorothy quizzed the guard. "Did you hear Royal Head Commander Paul's speech?"

"Yes."

"From where?"

"Upstairs."

Pushing harder, the young woman continued, "You heard the whole speech?"

"Yes."

"There was no static?"

"None."

Gertrude then asked, "What did he say?"

"It was an interesting speech."

"Could you tell us any of the specifics?" inquired Dorothy. "Did he mention anything pertaining to political prisoners or citizen's rights?"

"Not that I can recall."

"Do you remember anything at all?" pushed Gert.

"No."

"But you just said it was an interesting speech?" Dorothy countered.

"It was."

"How can you say that if you don't remember any of the details?"

Dorothy continued, "Can't you tell us anything?"

Instead of answering, he started to clean the table. "This is not fair!" Dorothy shouted. "You're holding us here against our will. You offer us no logical reason for your behavior. Do you think we're just stupid and will accept this behavior without question?" Pushing harder, she asked, "Are you politically affiliated with anyone?"

"I'm not at liberty to say."

Gert stormed in, "Damnit! It's *our* lives that are affected by all of this, not yours! If you can't give us the answers we want, send in someone who can!"

As he turned to exit, he remarked, "You'll be leaving tomorrow." Both sat stunned, gazing at one another.

"Where are we going?" Gert finally asked.

"I'm not at liberty to say."

"How can you do such a thing to us?" Dorothy objected. Before she could say another word, he was gone from the room. The two women looked blankly at each other.

"Now what?" inquired Gert.

"God only knows," replied Dorothy.

"I guess we'll find out tomorrow." Neither could sleep, but reclined on their individual beds.

"Gert?"

"Yes, Dorothy."

"I'm frightened."

Gert looked at her young friend. "So am I. I'm scared to death."

"I guess we have to wait until tomorrow, don't we?"

Gertrude reached out and touched Dorothy's hand. "I just want to let you know I love you very much."

Dorothy sobbed, "I love you too, Gert. Very, very much."

Hearing the key turn in the lock the next morning, Dorothy moved to Gert's side. Holding hands, they apprehensively waited for the door to open. Four large men entered. "Are you ready?" one asked.

Squeezing Dorothy's hand, Gert replied, "Yes. We're ready." Positioning themselves between the four guards, they walked quietly to a waiting limousine. Once both were securely seated, the car pulled down the long driveway and onto the main roadway. After fifteen minutes of silence, Gertrude inquired, "Would it do any good to ask where we are going?"

"No." was the immediate, one-word response. Gert glanced at Dorothy. Their eyes met and the elderly woman could sense her friend's overpowering anxiety. She studied each man's expression for any clue or hint. Though they individually avoided her stares, they also seemed unusually uncomfortable. After making a sharp right turn onto a bumpy, dirt road, the limo came to a stop.

Gazing out the window, Gert watched as the driver exited the car and spoke to several armed guards. Moments later he returned and waited for the wrought-iron gate to open. The men signaled him ahead and then reclosed the gate as the car passed. Ahead, several large buildings loomed and as they drew nearer, armed guards appeared everywhere. Hundreds of men posted around the complex, stared as the vehicle drew closer. Rolling to a stop, the door opened and two of the guards exited. "Please get out," one demanded.

As the two women prepared to leave, Gertrude was held in place by the guard still sitting at her left. As Dorothy stood outside and waited for her friend to join her, the two men grasped her arms and restrained her.

"What are you doing? He wants us out," Gert said.

"No, just her."

"I will not stay, I'm—" Her sentence was cut short as the door slammed shut. The vehicle pulled away. Dorothy, held stationary by her captors, stood and watched in horror.

"Where are you taking her?" she cried. "I thought it was over?"

Several other guards encircled the young woman. "Come," commanded one of the guards. Her discouraged body limply followed. What had been given back was once again retaken. After entering the building, they walked briskly down a lengthy corridor until they came to a heavy metal door. On either side, stood an armed guard. "You may go in." Without asking any questions, Dorothy opened the door and walked forward.

The sound of the door swinging inward caused everyone in the room to look.

"It's Dorothy!" a chorus of voices sung out. Her name was repeated over and over as the sound of footsteps filled the large hall. Gazing around the crowded area, tears flowed from Dorothy's eyes. Everything became blurred as her heart pounded wildly. Someone grabbed her and held her tightly. After turning her around, he began kissing her face.

Recognizing Austin's features, she returned his passion. "Austin, I've been so scared. My God, so worried!" They continued to hold one another as the rest of the staff surrounded their rediscovered friend.

A little while later, Dorothy explained her ordeal. "You mean she's really alive?" Austin asked.

"Yes, Austin. Gertrude is still very much alive."

"Why did they bring only you here?"

"I'm not sure, but there's much more to this whole thing than any of us ever suspected. I do believe Gertrude is a key player in the game."

"A key player? Do you think she's involved?"

"Not voluntarily, but somehow, she's an integral part of something really big. Call it intuition, but I sense it's definitely huge." They held hands and kissed. "I was so afraid I'd never see you again. I couldn't bear the thought," Dorothy said. As she kissed him near his ear, she whispered, "I love you, Austin Mathews."

"Please promise me you'll never leave my side again. I can't live without you," he replied.

Smiling she stated, "I can interpret that many different ways."

"If we ever get out of this mess, I'll make it much more official with a ring." He pulled her closer. "And that's a promise."

"I'll gladly accept the offer." They then joined the others to speculate on Gertrude's second disappearance—and their own future.

FIFTY - SIX

Meanwhile the limousine pulled up to the front of another complex of buildings. Walking between her kidnappers, Gert observed armed men everywhere. Knowing better than to ask, she remained silent and followed her captives' lead. Once inside, they were stopped by three sentries. Addressing Gert, one of her captors spoke: "Go with them."

With no debate, she followed his orders. They led her to the lower level of the building and down a long, well-lit hallway. At the end stood a heavy oak door. They opened the door and stepped aside for her to enter.

Sitting at the far end of a long conference table was a tall, bearded man. Recognizing the stranger immediately, Gertrude ran to his side. Despite herself, she embraced him briefly, "I'm so happy to see you. Thank goodness they didn't hurt you. I was so distraught when I didn't find you in the park and when they brought me *Moby Dick*, I thought those men had killed you."

Looking downward at her, he softly spoke, "I'm just fine, Miss Johnson. Everything is all right. Your ordeal is over."

One of the two guards asked, "Will you be needing anything

else Royal Head Commander Paul?"

The words echoed through the room.

Gertrude stepped back and looked up into his eyes. Meekly, she asked, "Is it true?"

"Yes, Gertrude, it is." Turning to his men, he ordered, "You may leave us." After the door had closed, the two people sat. Gert wrung her hands nervously, "I'm afraid I don't understand any of this."

"It's actually quite complex."

"Why didn't you tell me who you were?"

"It was not possible."

"I'm very confused."

Tenderly, he began his tale, "My father had been very sick for a long time."

"But all the stories and broadcasts didn't say anything about it.... In fact they only mentioned how well he was and of his exploits," Gertrude interceded.

"All lies and fabrications. He'd been confined to a bed for the past year. A stroke left him paralyzed and unable to speak. I was studying abroad when it struck. When I heard the news, I immediately returned home to be at his side."

"Why did you come to my bookstore?"

"I believe the answer is quite obvious: I love reading books."

"And mine was the only place to buy them?"

"Well, I went to Schnieders' until they came under close scrutiny; I had to keep a low profile for obvious reasons." He continued, "When General Daniels and his followers assumed control of the government, he caught me by surprise and at my most vulnerable time when I was grieving the death of my father."

"How did you regain your position?"

"The timing had to be just right for my restoration of power. I had to make sure it could be done quickly and without any bloodshed. In essence, I had to wait for a quick and bloodless solution."

"So it was General Daniels who instituted all the unreasonable changes?"

"Yes. My father was incapable of governing; therefore, the General grasped the opportunity and assumed control. Everything autocratic was his doing; unfortunately I was powerless at the time to prevent any of it from occurring."

"Why did he kidnap me?"

"He didn't. I had you and your staff taken."

"You? Why?"

"For your protection. When I received the illegal, new books from you, I knew it was only a matter of time before the General found out. I knew he would forcibly attack and close your building, so I had my men beat him to the punch. The move saved your entire staff and you from his clutches."

"What about my books?"

"My men went to your store and PAT's cave and removed everything. It's all been safely stored and protected."

"Where are Dorothy, Austin, and the rest of my staff?"

"All safe and protected from the General."

"Why couldn't you just tell me about all of this?"

"Two reasons: If it backfired, you'd be killed as a traitor of the state, and secondly, I had to complete the overthrow of the General's interim regime."

"Was it successful?"

"Yes. It went smoother than expected. My troops are in full control of every aspect of the government."

"What about me?"

"You will be reunited with everyone after a meeting."

"What meeting?"

"I will be addressing the entire nation tomorrow evening. I will need you to assist me in the finalization of my plans."

"Me? I'm not a politician."

"You and several others will have considerable influence in my policy making. My father's policies and those of General Daniel's must be buried forever. We must create fresh ideas for all.

Individual freedom must be restored to my country and to my people. That is why I need your help. You are a wise woman. You are
a gifted leader and highly respected among your peers." Looking
her in the eye, the Commander asked, "Please, Gertrude Johnson.
Please help me redirect and establish my new government."

"I can't believe any of this is for real," Gertrude mused.

"It's for real. I need your help. If you want independence and
freedom for your fellow citizens, then share with me your wisdom
and assistance."

Realizing Paul had described everything she had been working
for, Gertrude relented, "I accept the position."

He pressed the intercom. "Tell my cabinet to please come in."
When introductions were concluded, the group undertook the
Royal Head Commander's challenge. With his approval and full
support, Gertrude Johnson and the others created a national policy
based on liberty, human rights, freedom, and democracy. Using her
tremendous cultural and literary background, the elderly bookstore
proprietor helped mold her country's optimistic future.

FIFTY-SEVEN

As the nation's masses huddled around their radios, the final preparations were taking place behind the scenes. Dorothy adjusted Gertrude's new dress, then put the finishing touches on her freshly cut hair. "How do I look?" asked Gert.

"You look just sensational. I just can't believe this is all happening," Dorothy said.

"There isn't time for such talk; where's Austin?"

"He's in the studio with the rest of the staff."

Holding Dorothy close, Gert said, "I'm so happy for you and Austin."

"I'm sure we'll be happy together," replied Dorothy.

"I knew it would end this way for the two of you. It was predestined."

"And if the bookstore doesn't work out," Dorothy laughed. "You could always open a marriage brokerage business."

"One match a lifetime is my limit." Looking at her watch, Gertrude commented, "We'd better be going. We don't want to keep our country waiting."

Royal Head Commander Paul stood at the podium, with the

studio lights brightly shining; he wiped his forehead with a small, white handkerchief. He glanced anxiously around the room and mentally prepared himself for his first public speech. Though he had practiced it many times during the earlier part of the day, fear and reality were both settling in. He watched the director signal, "Three, two, one. You're on the air."

"I come to you, my people, as your new and magnanimous leader. I am prepared to undertake the colossal and awesome responsibility of Royal Head Commander for our great country. I accept this honor just as my father and our entire lineage has done during the course of our nation's distinguished history. Before I go on, however, I would like to publicly thank General Daniels and his entire staff for assisting me during a most difficult period. My personal grief over the death of my father must be postponed; I must dedicate my life to you, my fellow citizens."

Shifting his position slightly, he spoke slowly and distinctly. Each word had been deliberately and carefully selected for the occasion: "During the next few months, each of you will experience sweeping changes. We, the greatest nation on the earth, will and must modify our prevailing policies, procedures, and methodologies. New reforms must occur. You will have a greater say in the formation of your own destiny. I have already implemented several alterations to expedite these changes. Within one year, I am recommending the reinstatement of public elections. My newly appointed cabinet has already begun work on this critical project.

"A refashioning of our entire government will occur. Other aspects will also be ..." After nearly an hour of speaking, Royal Head Commander Paul asked his cabinet ministers to stand and introduce themselves. "At this time, I would like to ask a very special woman and close advisor to come forward and say a few words." Gertrude, who was seated on the dais next to Rebecca, Samuel, and Stephen, now stood and walked nervously to the podium. Royal Head Commander Paul adjusted the microphone, squeezed her hand for reassurance, and then stepped backward so Gertrude Johnson became the focal point of the nation's attention.

She glanced at her notes, nervously coughed once, and then began her speech: "Royal Head Commander Paul, distinguished cabinet members, illustrious advisors, and citizens of this magnificent country, today marks a monumental benchmark in our nation's history." Holding up the last copy of the Gutenberg Bible, she continued. "This Bible was the first book to ever be printed from movable type. It has withstood the test of time. Despite many contrasting forms of government, dictatorships, and monarchies, it has endured both physically and in concept. It should, therefore, be a symbol for each of us to emulate. The printed page has once again reentered your lives."

The camera shifted to Rebecca, Samuel, and Stephen as Gert said, "Along with these three courageous and qualified individuals, I will make sure your freedom and privilege of choice will be restored. Never allow yourselves the opportunity to lose it again, for knowledge is the foundation of your society and the building block of your cultural history. Without this privilege, each of you will become a lemming. I trust, with all my heart, that our country's future will be as bright and optimistic as I anticipate." Opening the Bible, she translated the first three words. "'In the beginning'...My fellow countrymen, this is our new beginning."

Upon the completion of their speeches, Royal Head Commander Paul, Gertrude, and the others seated on the dais answered questions from the media.

"When do you expect these freedoms to actually begin?"

"Yesterday," jested Paul. "They already have. The station from which this broadcast is originating is no longer government-owned or operated. I have given full control to its administration. Within several months, the public should have at least three more independent channels from which to select their programs—none of which shall be government manipulated or directed."

They asked Rebecca, "What role shall you play?"

"I will be an advisor to those who require my expertise. Since the government will no longer control the printed page, I'll be here to help the magazine industry prosper and flourish once more."

"Stephen, will you continue to deal with pornography?"

"I will restrict my business to my very first love: I am an art dealer. That does not mean, however, that I personally condemn any type of printed material. In a free society, every citizen must have the right to read what he or she wishes."

"What about newspapers?"

Samuel responded: "Several dailies are being launched. Each and every one will be privately owned and operated."

"How can the four of you handle all the work?"

Gertrude answered, "Our staffs are well trained, highly educated, and deeply motivated. They will travel throughout our country and help where needed. This, however, must be a grassroots movement; you cannot rely solely on us. Each citizen has been given what was originally theirs; it is now up to them to savor its sweetness."

After the interview was terminated, everyone went to the Capital Building for an elaborate celebration party.

FIFTY-EIGHT

Later the next day, a car pulled into the small cemetery. Gertrude, Austin, and Dorothy climbed out and walked slowly to the three grave sites. They stood silently for several minutes, before Gertrude placed a tiny rose on each plot. Smiling, she touched Silas' headstone. "Yes, Silas. You were right. Together we could do it." Dorothy and Austin pulled Gertrude into their arms. Today's tears were shed for joy, life, and hope. After awhile, Gertrude spoke again. "It's time to go. The new beginning awaits us."

And it came to pass
that Gertrude and the others were triumphant.
The new beginning was successful,
and the printed page endured...

Other books by Stanley L. Alpert

MOHOP MOGANDE

THE SWAN SONG PENTAD

A ROOMFUL OF PARADOX

Available from

Alpert's Bookery, Inc.
POB 215
Nanuet, NY 10954

E. M. Berger

About the Author

Stanley L. Alpert is the author of *Mohop Mogande, The Swan Song Pentad,* and *A Roomful of Paradox.* He has two goals: to contribute to humankind through writing about controversial and ethical challenges; and to write 100 books by his 100th birthday. Mr. Alpert lives with his wife and daughter in the state of New York.